Tears of the Dragon

Ryan McGinnis

Text Copyright © 2021 by Ryan McGinnis

978-0-578-33182-9 (paperback)

ryan-mcginnis.com

For Amber,
who has always thought it was a good idea
for me to write a story.

CHAPTER ONE

End of the Chase

Marcus Jamali sat in the oppressive heat of an Arizona morning fingering the road dirt on the dashboard of his black SUV. He hated this place, the heat, the dirt, the blinding sun, but the dust was the worst. The air-conditioning had died a few days ago so they had been riding around in the blazing heat, up and down the highways with the windows down. That combined with the dry conditions had covered the inside of the truck with a thick layer of dust. He reached for his water bottle, checked to find it empty, and chucked it into the floorboard. As miserable as he was, Marcus felt lucky. The individual they had been in pursuit of had managed to lose them. Because of that, they had wandered around in the god-forsaken desert for the last two days. Just when his crew had started getting antsy they had gotten the call that their target had been spotted in Wingfield, Arizona. Soon after they had arrived in town, set up surveillance, and soon had him in their sights. Now with any luck they could wrap this up and get back on schedule.

While waiting he watched across the street as an old man locked up an ancient, dilapidated garage. The structure, much like the man, seemed to sag and sink in an eternal state of submission. The man, breathing heavily, locked the door and stuck the keys in his dingy coveralls before wandering to his late model car and driving away.

"So this is what the American Dream has come down to?" thought Marcus.

"Poor bastard, worked all his life and what does he get? Ground down by the machine. At the end of it all he's left with poor health and a business that can't survive the reckless economic greed. A couple of days ago we had the solution. A couple of days ago we could have relieved the suffering and set it right. But then he showed up and ruined it." Marcus paused at the thought of the stranger, who had shown up out of the blue and snatched away their achievement at the very cusp of victory. The mere thought of him and the trouble he had caused them made his blood boil.

Just then, he received a text that their target should be coming into his line of sight anytime now. Marcus looked around at the dilapidated, mostly abandoned, warehouses around them. They had picked the perfect area for this to go down. Once a busy industrial section, this side of town had seen hard times and was now full of abandoned buildings and shells of former bustling industry. He looked down the street and immediately saw their target. You couldn't miss him honestly. Despite the heat the slender figure was dressed in a black suit and a skinny necktie. Between the suit and his slick hair Marcus figured he looked like an extra from a mobster movie. He moved quickly down the street with a duffle bag slung over his arm. The thought he might actually be carrying what they were looking for in the duffle bag disappointed Marcus. This man had led them on a chase across the Southwestern United States and nothing would make Marcus happier than to have to 'interrogate' him to find out where he had hidden their property.

Suddenly, the stranger veered off course and crossed a short parking lot. He stopped in front of an old warehouse, fidgeted with the lock and then opened the door. He stopped for a second to look back at the street and then slipped inside and shut the door. Immediately Marcus and his team sprang out of the SUV and moved across the street, where they were met in the alleyway by Victor and Peter, who had been tailing their target through town on foot.

"I've checked the back exit, it's chained shut. This is the only way in or out," said Victor.

Marcus nodded "Okay this is how it goes down, we use small ordinance only. Do not shoot unless you have to, we want him alive. We hit the front door, split up and take him down." The other five men nodded and checked their earpieces and sidearms. On Marcus' signal they quietly opened the door and rushed inside.

Dust hung heavily in the air and coated everything inside the old warehouse. The smell of mold, decay, and rotting wood filled the place. They hung back in the dark shadows of the dimly lit warehouse letting their eyes adjust. Marcus knew that their prey must know they were inside. He was in here somewhere hiding, but Marcus wouldn't rush it, this had been a long, miserable chase and he was going to relish finally reaching the end of the trail. He signaled the other five to spread out and each take an aisle. They would continue the sweep until they flushed him out, then the real fun could begin.

Marcus slowly made his way down the aisle between the tall shelves. Each shelf was covered in a variety of old industrial equipment. Between the junk all over the place and the dim light from the dirty skylights, Marcus could barely see. Suddenly Victor's voice came over his earpiece, "Marcus, we got a problem!"

Marcus barked back "Maintain radio silence! You know the drill!"

Victor's voice came back quieter this time, "Peter's dead."

Moments later Marcus stood with Victor over Peter's body. Victor was crouched over the body looking it over with his flashlight.

"Broken neck" said Victor as he swept his light over the lifeless body that had minutes ago been their comrade.

Marcus snorted "What the hell? Pete's a professional, no way that Las Vegas reject got the jump on him."

Suddenly the silence of the dusty warehouse was shattered by two gun shots. Marcus and Victor raced toward the sound of the gunfire and couldn't believe the sight they found. Two more bodies were laying in the aisle. Blood slowly seeping from the gunshot wounds in their heads. Just past the bodies they saw the stranger, his back to them, with some sort of cable or cord wrapped around the only other member of their team left. Marcus hit the spotlight on the end of his gun, illuminating the stranger's pale skin.

"Don't move! Let him go!" screamed Marcus.

The stranger glanced over his shoulder but showed no sign of letting up. Marcus nodded to Victor and they both closed in on the target, fingers tightening on the trigger as they approached. Suddenly, at almost the precise moment their fingers squeezed the trigger, the stranger spun with incredible speed so that their shots hit their own man in the chest. Marcus could only stare in horror as the man dropped to the ground. The stranger had vanished.

"What the hell? Nobody is that fast!" Victor moved forward, sweeping his light back and forth.

"Wait!" said Marcus, but it was too late. There was a sudden movement in the shadows off to Victor's right. Marcus heard what sounded like metal slicing through the air and Victor suddenly dropped to the ground in a heap. In the dim light Marcus saw something roll across the floor toward him. When he played his light down he saw Victor's head at his feet. Marcus felt panic well up inside him, as he stumbled backwards away from his partner's severed head. He swung his light to the right and suddenly the stranger appeared in front of him, his steely eyes staring a hole in Marcus. Before he could squeeze the trigger, there was a flash of metal in the flashlight beam. The flashlight wobbled wildly, throwing the beam all over the room. Marcus tried to steady it but couldn't. He glanced at it and saw his gun hand falling to the floor. He heard the slicing sound again and suddenly everything started to fade. Briefly Marcus felt the sensation of falling and drifting past himself and then all was dark.

Xavier Greene stood over the body of Marcus Jamali, watching the blood pour from the stump of his neck. It oozed across the floor in the dim light, slowly filling the cracks in the old wooden floor. He reached down and turned off the spotlight on the gun. Then, moving quickly, he picked up a rag and wiped the blade of his katana clean. Reaching back, he slid the sword up into the holster that he wore on his back under his jacket. When the blade was as far as it went the tang compressed allowing the katana to shorten further and fit under his jacket. Xavier looked at the chaos around him. He didn't have time to clean up, even in this abandoned part of the city someone may have heard the gunshots and he would have to leave the area immediately and get back to his true hideout. He quickly retrieved his duffle bag from a random shelf among the junk and started toward the front door. He paused for a moment, looking back at the warehouse and opened the door. The sunlight immediately blinded him and before his eyes could adjust he heard "Freeze! Yavapai County Sheriff Department!"

Xavier blinked his eyes, trying to adjust to the bright sunlight. As his sight recovered he saw three young, thin deputies and an older, overweight Sheriff, his considerable bulk threatening to bust the buttons on the shirt of his uniform.

"May I help you officers?" said Xavier, eyeing the officers.

The rotund sheriff stepped forward "I'm Sheriff Fredrick Thompson, we're responding to reports of gunfire in the area, is this your building?"

"No, I'm afraid not. I'm a building inspector, Xavier Greene, hired to look this place over. It's in really bad shape, I'm afraid."

The sheriff eyed Xavier wearily, "Like every other building on this block, if the city had the money they would probably tear this whole place down." He looked Xavier over carefully, "Say, you're not from around here are you?"

"No, I'm from back east, just traveling with work. You know how it goes in this economy." Xavier offered up the best smile he could muster.

"Well, fair enough," replied the sheriff, "mind if I take a look around before you lock it up?"

"Of course, feel free." Xavier replied.

As the sheriff walked slowly into the warehouse Xavier felt a tightness growing in his stomach. His mission was important and he could easily take out the rookie deputies and sheriff but he had always been against harming the innocent, and even though these officers were in his way, they were merely doing their duties. Just then a young deputy approached Xavier.

"Hi I'm Deputy Culpepper, you can call me Jimmy." Xavier smiled weakly and shook his hand. "I'm sorry for the inconvenience, I'm sure we'll have you on your way in no—"

Suddenly they heard a crashing sound and the Sheriff burst from the warehouse. "HOLY SHIT!" exclaimed the Sheriff, panting and wiping his now heavily sweating brow. He pulled his gun and pointed it at Xavier. "Sheriff, what the hell is going on?" asked Jimmy, clearly perplexed.

"Get back, get away from him!" stammered the sheriff. "Get your hands up!"

Xavier dropped his duffle bag to the ground and calmly lifted his hands. The Sheriff instructed Jimmy to cuff Xavier, while the other two deputies went through his bag.

"I'm sure I can explain everything, officer," said Xavier as he calmly allowed Jimmy to place the cuffs on him. Jimmy searched Xavier and pulled a pair of knives from his jacket, as well as a pouch containing a pack of pills, a cable hidden in the arm of his jacket, and the sword hidden behind his back.

"Are you sure about that?" asked the sheriff. "You have the right to remain silent and in my opinion, from the looks of things, and what I found in that warehouse, it would be in your best interest to do so."

CHAPTER TWO

In the Jail House Now

An hour later, Sheriff Fredrick Thompson and his deputies huddled around the desk in their office trying to get their heads wrapped around the situation that they had stumbled into.

Jimmy watched the sheriff fidget with the paperwork, going endlessly over the details. Personally he had never seen anything like what they saw on the inside of that warehouse. Wingfield was a small town after all. Jaywalking and the occasional drunken fight between tourists were about the biggest things to ever happen. And the tourists were another problem entirely. If word got out about a massacre it might hurt the town's reputation and the valuable tourist dollars that flowed in. It was at moments like this that Jimmy was glad he was just a deputy and not the sheriff.

Sheriff Fredrick Thompson mopped his red balding head. He could feel the beads of sweat running down. As long as he could remember he broke out in a steady sweat at the slightest hint of stress. Truthfully he had never dealt with it very well. When he was young he had managed to get a job working for the Las Vegas Police department, a move that at the time seemed like a really good idea. It soon became apparent that he wasn't cut out for the Las Vegas life as his anxiety got worse, which only exacerbated his glandular condition. Fortunately he found an opening in the small town of Wingfield, Arizona and resigned his position in Vegas soon thereafter. Since then he had developed a fine department in this sleepy tourist town. But now he looked around the room and knew that these young deputies were in way over their heads. As far as he knew he was in way over his head as well but decisions had to be made and unfortunately it was up to him. He sat and watched the deputies chatter amongst themselves and finally cleared his throat to quiet the room.

"Okay listen up, I know you're all rattled and frankly I am too, but we'll get through this as long as we keep our heads. Now, we've left John guarding the scene but so far I have not informed the mayor, in fact the warehouse is just locked with a car sitting out front."

Jimmy spoke up, "Isn't that against regulations?"

The Sheriff shot Jimmy a look that froze him in his tracks

"Damn straight it is, but I would say this whole situation is pretty out of the ordinary. Honestly, we've never had anything like this happen in this town and we're gonna have to be careful and handle this whole thing delicately. Now I plan on calling the State Police in to process the crime scene because we're not equipped to handle anything of that magnitude."

"Why the State Police? Why not the feds?" interjected Jimmy, much to the Sheriff's annoyance.

"Because the State Police are personal friends of mine and they'll be more open to the delicateness of the situation. You see, we're gonna have to do our best to keep this as quiet as possible. I know the Mayor, and I know for a fact that if our tourism takes a hit because of this, we'll all be looking for a job!"

The Sheriff looked from deputy to deputy trying to read their faces. In his opinion it was unorthodox, but given the situation he felt like it was the best way to balance the situation with respect to what was gonna be the mayor's number one concern, the flow of tourist and more importantly, the flow of tourist dollars into Wingfield.

"Okay, that's the drill, if nobody has anything else to add, I'm going to head over to the Mayor's office and start the unfortunate task of informing him about the incident and how we're gonna handle it. Jimmy if you will, call Byron at the State Po-"

"Pardon me, if I may make a simple suggestion, I believe we can clear this whole thing up."

The entire room turned slowly and stared at the ghostly pale, thin figure sitting in the holding cell. Since being read his rights, he had been quiet, complacent and calm, almost to the point of being eerie. Now as the Sheriff stared at the black suited figure in the cell something else made him uneasy. When they had put him in the cell the Sheriff was sure that his hands had been handcuffed behind his back. Now he sat with his still cuffed hands in his lap, like he was waiting for his name to be called at a doctor's office.

"What did you say?" asked the Sheriff, sure that he had heard him, but just wanting more time to process it.

Xavier spoke again, "I believe I can assist you in clearing up this whole situation and help you 'keep a lid on it' at the same time."

"And just how would you do that?"

"Simple" replied Xavier, "I am allowed one phone call, am I not?"

The Sheriff stared incredulously at the figure in the cell and suddenly broke into a huge belly laugh.

"You've got to be kidding me!" the Sheriff roared, "How stupid do you think I am? Suppose I let you use the phone, next thing I know, your boss has sent a bunch of hired killers in here to clean up your mess. No thanks, I had enough of you mafia types up in Vegas."

Xavier continued to study the man with his calm grey eyes "Sheriff, I assure you, that even though I cannot tell you exactly what I am, you can trust me. One call to clarify this whole situation is all that I'm asking. The longer we stall, the greater the risk that someone else will show up, and trust me, if more do show up, that warehouse will be the least of your problems."

The deputies looked back at the Sheriff, who was standing with his mouth agape. He could feel his back drenched in sweat, blood vessels were bulging from his temples. Slowly he processed what he had just heard. Finally he said "Supposing I do let you make a phone call, just who do you plan on calling?"

Xavier paused a second or two and replied "The Federal Bureau of Investigation regional office in Flagstaff, Arizona."

The Sheriff slowly turned his gaze from Xavier to his deputies and back. He could feel his anxiety level blowing through the roof. He was starting to feel that turning down retirement last year was a really bad idea.

At long last, the Sheriff picked up a grabber used to pick up trash and gripped the receiver of his phone with it. He walked over to the holding cell and extended the stick with the receiver out to Xavier.

Xavier stared at the stick and the Sheriff before finally taking the receiver from him. The Sheriff calmly walked back to his desk and sat down beside the phone.

"For the record, I think this is a really bad idea, but I'm willing to entertain it on the slim chance that you are some type of government agent and not some psycho serial killer. Now, if you don't mind, I'll get the number myself."

Sheriff Thompson filed through his numbers till he found the number for the FBI's Flagstaff office. He hit speaker phone, dialed the main line and the directory soon came over the receiver requesting the parties extension number. The Sheriff looked at Xavier impatiently.

"1146." said Xavier.

The Sheriff punched in the extension and the phone began to ring. The phone was answered by a voice with a thick Texas accent. "Special Agent Bill Logan."

"Agent Logan, this is Yavapai County Sheriff Fredrick Thompson. I have a suspect who requested to be patched through to you." With that the Sheriff turned off the speakerphone and nodded at Xavier, who lifted the receiver to his ear.

Xavier quickly spoke "Agent Logan, my name is Xavier Greene, I was instructed you would be my liaison if I needed assistance while in this area."

Xavier could hear the click of computer keys in the background, "Let me see, yep here you are all right. Hmm, that's strange, usually I have a whole case file when I'm expected to assist someone but all it has is your name, not even an ID number. You must be of high importance to be classified past my level. But I guess that's none of my business." he mused, "So what can I do for you Mr. Greene?"

Xavier replied "I'm in Wingfield Arizona, passing through on 'business'. This morning there was an incident and the Sheriff happened to witness the aftermath. So now I'm sitting in a holding cell in the Sheriff's office. I need you to convince him that it would be in his best interest to allow me to continue on my way."

There was a pause "Baaahahahahahahaha! Are you serious? You're apparently so classified that I can't access your info and you got caught by the Wingfield Sheriff's department? Oh man, I hope you appreciate the irony of the situation."

Xavier stared at the phone in disbelief, he had never heard such a rude, unprofessional person in his entire life.

Finally, Logan calmed down and spoke again "Okay, sorry about that, I'm sure it's not as funny to you. I was just giving you a hard time. I'll be glad to speak to the Sheriff and get him to let you go."

Xavier heard someone in the background speak to Agent Logan. Suddenly he spoke again "Xavier, do you mind if I put you on hold for a second?"

Xavier started to reply but the line had already clicked to

background music. He sat, trying to hide his annoyance. Finally he heard Agent Logan pick up again.

"Xavier, change of plans. I'm gonna come down there personally to get you released. I figure it's the least I can do after offending you."

"That will hardly be necessary Agent Logan. Time is of the essence, I must be allowed to go as soon as possible." Xavier replied.

"I understand that," Logan continued, "but that's the way it's gonna have to be. Don't worry, it should only take me about two hours to get down there. Sit tight, okay?"

"Fine," replied Xavier, "just be here as quickly as you can. I don't have long."

"You got it," came the reply. "Now just put me on the phone with the Sheriff. Thanks."

Xavier held out the receiver, only for the Sheriff to once again use the grabber to take the phone from him. He cradled the phone to his ear as he huddled back over behind his desk.

"I see, yes, I understand. You've gotta be kidding me?" The Sheriff paused for a second to turn and look at Xavier and then turned his back and continued, "Well yeah I understand that. But you gotta know I'm not letting him go unless I see some type of paperwork. No, you didn't see what I saw in that warehouse. I'm definitely gonna need some type of official clearance before I let him go anywhere."

After another minute of muttering into the phone, the Sheriff hung up and turned to face the holding cell.

"Well, I'll be a son of a bitch. Seems our friend here does have something to do with the government, although nobody will apparently fill me in on exactly what he does. I was just told to keep him comfortable until the Agent shows up to escort him. Jimmy, give the man a water."

Jimmy used the grabber stick and handed Xavier a bottle of water through the bars. "What about the crime scene?" He asked.

The Sheriff replied "According to our friend from the FBI, they will send someone down to clean it up and we're not to worry about it any further. In other words, until the Feds get here, we wait."

The Sheriff sank back into his chair and looked at Xavier. "I don't know who you are but once this guy gets here and springs you, I expect you to hit the road and never look back, do I make myself clear?"

"Crystal clear, Sheriff." replied Xavier. He then turned and returned to his cot in the cell. Something was clearly off with the FBI agent, but there was little he could do about it. For now there was only one thing to do. Xavier's last few weeks had been a whirlwind and he had hardly had time to breathe, much less process all that he had been through in such a short time. Slowly he sat down on the cot and drew his legs up into a lotus position. He slowed his breathing and began to allow himself to drift away into the mist of his mind, purposefully relaxing and allowing his thoughts to travel back a few weeks to the start of the mission...

CHAPTER THREE

A Look Back

Several Weeks earlier...

The wind billowed the snow in swirls down from the high cliffs of the Himalayas through the canyon. The storm had stopped hours ago but with the fierce winds it seemed to perpetually be snowing. If you stared close enough you would notice whiffs of smoke mixed in with the swirling snow. If you were lucky enough to trace it all the way down to its source, you would find a hidden monastery on the cliff side. In a remote section of the mountains, far off the beaten path, far from the commercial hiking routes and known only to a few outside sherpas, the mysterious Bhuti Ling Monastery guarded its secrets well. As if the remote location wasn't enough, high walls and locked gates reinforced the notion that this was not a place of welcome to outsiders. The monks there followed a strict code of rules, not the least of which was strict isolation from the outside world. However there are exceptions to every rule even at Bhuti Ling. For in a room deep in the monastery sat Xavier Greene.

The room was dimly lit by a single candle in the center of the room. Xavier sat in the lotus position on the hardwood floors focused entirely on the candle. His hands worked furiously forming various shapes and contortions that together made up the 'nine symbolic cuts' of the Kuji-Kiri, a mysterious meditation technique known only to a few. It is said that when done properly this technique would open up nine energy structures, enabling the user to be at one with the matrix of the world. When one masters this power it is said that you could potentially increase your willpower, quickness of mind and body, and reflexes exponentially. Quan-Li, Xavier's friend and teacher, had told him that he will know he has mastered the technique when the flame appears to stop flickering and freeze in time. Xavier had worked furiously at the technique for months but to no avail. He knew there were monks in the temple who were angry at Quan-Li for sharing this secret with an 'outsider'. Indeed, it was said that the technique was never meant for anyone, except a true monk of Bhuti Ling. However, Quan-Li was the grandmaster, so his word was law. He had decreed that Xavier could stay there, so he was there. He concentrated on the flame, indeed the entire world had ceased to exist outside of the candle. The flame danced tauntingly as Xavier continued over and over through the nine cuts. Finally he thought he saw the candle slow just slightly. Could it be progress after all this time? Suddenly the gong tolled, signaling the end of the evening meditations. At once the flame flickered on as if nothing happened, before a monk came out of the darkness and snuffed the candle out, while another lit the lamps around the room. Xavier sat for a few moments more before rising, taking a sip of water, and beginning the long walk back to his quarters.

As he walked Xavier thought back on the generosity that Quan-Li had bestowed upon him, indeed if it hadn't been for Quan-Li, he would be dead. When he was younger, Xavier had been recruited by the Citadel, a power conglomeration of influential people, corporations and even countries that operated in the shadows. No one knew exactly what the Citadel did, but their influence spanned the globe and rarely was a major policy decision made anywhere without their input. Originally, Xavier had served primarily as an assassin, taking out assigned targets without questioning. But as the years went by his grace under pressure and problem solving skills had allowed him to become a more specialized tool. In time, he became known in the intelligence community as 'the Silencer', a highly specialized agent who had the ability to seemingly appear and disappear without a trace. Eventually, he was only sent on the most important and high stakes missions, which afforded him better paydays and less of a work schedule. Then, on one fateful mission, things went wrong. Xavier was attempting to secure a hard drive containing sensitive information that would have changed the balance of power in the free world. The Citadel did not approve of the balance shifting and had sent Xavier to make sure it didn't happen. In the end he intercepted the hard drive but during the ensuing chase was trapped in an avalanche in the Himalayas. The Citadel had sent search parties but assumed he was dead. In actuality, Quan-Li had happened upon his body near the monastery. He had taken him in, against the wishes of the other monks and nursed him back to health. Quan-Li had urged him to give up his job and stay with the monks, but Xavier felt he could look out for the greater good, even in the role that life had cast him. So he sent the hard drive to a Citadel safe house along with a letter telling them that he had been convalescing from injuries, but that he was alive and willing to return to work on two conditions. The first condition was that his location remain anonymous. When he was needed for a mission a package was to be sent to a village in the Himalayas. A messenger would then take the package to Xavier's true location, and he would respond. His second condition was that if they ever sent him a mission and he didn't respond, they were to consider him retired. Of course, the Citadel didn't like the terms, but after some negotiation, and in recognition of all the excellent work he had performed for them, they agreed. Since then Xavier had been sent two missions and had accepted both of them, to Quan-Li's chagrin. However, he hated to admit it, but more and more the old monk was getting to him and he found himself actually considering the life of isolation and mediation that he never thought would be for him. Each mission had gotten harder to accept and he had secretly been telling himself that each one would be his last.

When Xavier arrived at his room, he lit his lamp and immediately saw the padded envelope on his desk. He stared at the envelope long and hard before turning his attention to making a fire. He stood and stoked the fire until it was roaring nicely before he finally turned his attention back to the table. He approached the envelope and picked it up gingerly, as if afraid to touch it. He turned it over in his hands several times, contemplating throwing it into the fire and turning his back on the world forever. He stood holding the envelope for what seemed like an eternity until finally he sighed and ripped open the end. He poured the contents out onto the desk. Inside was exactly the same contents as always, a dossier folder containing info about the mission, and a small phone. For a second he thought about peeking at the dossier to discern whether he wanted to be part of the mission or not, but ultimately decided he had come this far, he may as well see it through. He turned on the phone and waited.

Approximately two minutes went by when the phone suddenly started to ring. Xavier answered it and immediately heard the cheerful voice of his handler, David on the other end of the phone.

"Xavier! I was hoping you would postpone retirement for another day!" This greeting had become par for the course since Xavier had announced his 'semi-retirement'.

"Yes, I supposed I have one more in me," said Xavier, continuing what had become their routine opening monologue. "So tell me, what do you have for me this time?"

David replied "Well, I'll be honest, you're probably not going to like this one very much. Have you ever heard of the Brotherhood of the Dragon?"

"No, I don't tend to watch the news."

"I didn't suppose you did, but anyway, they are a radical activist organization, mostly low level stuff, fighting corporate greed, sabotage, stuff like that. Recently though, we received intel that they had started working on a higher level project. We're still trying to figure out where they got the funding, but they put together a team of scientists and geneticists and have apparently come up with a virus that they've named 'Tears of the Dragon'. Not a lot is known about the details of the virus, except that it is extremely resilient outside of the host and once the incubation period is over, death comes within 6 hours. The worst part is the fatality rate is supposedly close to ninety five percent. We've estimated that the virus could spread and affect the entire population of Earth. With the exception of the most isolated places it could mostly wipe out the human race within three months."

As David paused, Xavier rubbed his forehead, as he started to wish he had thrown the envelope into the fire.

Xavier spoke first "So they have a virus that could potentially wipe out most of the civilized population of the Earth? What do they plan to do with it? Hold the world for ransom? Force a country to release their political hostages? What's their angle?"

David's reply came slowly "They plan to release it."

Xavier was stunned. "What?"

"They plan to release it," David continued "as retribution for the greed and corruption that, in their opinion, has subjugated the human race. They plan to burn it down and hope that something better grows from the ashes."

Xavier sat down on a stool that he had pulled up to the table and lit another lamp. He pulled the folder over and started going through it. "And how do I fit into this?" asked Xavier, although he already suspected the answer to that question.

"Your mission is to track down the Brotherhood and retrieve every sample of the virus, at all cost. Once recovered, you will take the virus to a lab location that will be provided to you and the virus is to be incinerated. The folder you have in front of you has all the information we have on the Brotherhood and their money trails. You'll need to start immediately."

"I can't leave until the morning," replied Xavier. "How long do I have before they plan on releasing it?"

The reply was not what he wanted to hear, "That's the thing, we're not sure. We have all of our contacts working on it, but there is a chance that they are already in motion. You're going to have to play serious catch up."

Xavier groaned, "Okay, I'll get to work on this immediately, see what else you can find out in the meantime. I'll check in when I get to a safe house."

"Thanks Xavier, I'll send you more information as it comes in, good luck."

With that Xavier turned the phone off and rubbed his eyes. Ideally Xavier had his missions thoroughly planned before he executed it, but this case was going to be different. He was going to be extremely rushed and he didn't like it. Being in a hurry leads to mistakes and in this business mistakes were frequently fatal.

After poring over the files for several hours he stoked the fire and began packing his supplies. He pulled his sword from its special case and checked it to make sure everything was in working order. The Citadel had given him a special katana, with a collapsible tang, which compressed in on itself to allow him to carry the sword undetected underneath his jacket. Of course, that wouldn't work going through an airport, so they had given him another gift, a box that when ran through the X-ray machine would appear to be just rolled up building plans.

When everything was ready he wrote a note to Quan-Li and stuck it on his door. He knew the old master would be unhappy that he had chosen to go battle the world once more, but to Xavier this time was different. To him this mission was a fight to save the fate of the people of the world. If the virus wasn't stopped countless innocents would be slaughtered and he couldn't allow that to happen. After he had pinned the note to his door he ventured down to find transport to the nearest village on what was going to be the start of a long journey indeed.

CHAPTER FOUR

Masaya

It was a crisp, clear evening in Lhasa, the administrative capital and second largest city in the Tibetan Autonomous Region. The name Lhasa literally means "place of the gods", and Xavier could see why as he sat staring out the window of his hotel room at the historic Banak Shöl Hotel. He glanced back at his laptop, awaiting the arrival of his "tech support", a hacker that he only knew by the name Stephen. He had worked with Stephen for several years now and he had proven himself an invaluable resource. Xavier also liked the fact that Stephen was not affiliated with the Citadel, as Xavier had kept him on his payroll and separate from his employer. He considered him an "ace in the hole", so to speak, a private resource who he could count on no matter what. Xavier smiled as he thought about the fact that one of the people he trusted the most was someone he had never met face to face. Now he sat waiting, attempting to be patient, despite the looming deadline that hung over his head. He had sent out an encrypted message to Stephen when he arrived in town and was anxious to see what he had uncovered. As if on cue, his laptop sprang to life, while at the same time his phone began ringing. Xavier took a sip of water and answered the phone.

"Hello Stephen, what do you have for me?" said Xavier, hoping that Stephen could give him an edge in this extremely urgent situation.

Stephen's voice burst through the phone, "Hi Xavier, well I have to admit, you put me in a real pressure cooker this time. Real fate of the world type stuff, no pressure right?"

Xavier was thrown off by the initial banter, "So are you saying that it's too much for you?"

"Quite the contrary," came the reply. "I haven't been this hype to do a job for you since that deal in Moscow a couple years ago! In any case, I've spent the last 16 hours going through all kinds of financial records. The thing is that the Brotherhood of the Dragon has always been a strictly small time group, mostly just protest and "occupy" type stuff. But suddenly 2 years ago they stepped it up exponentially. It's like they suddenly got some major backing. They started recruiting scientists and geneticists from all over the world to work on a secret project."

"Yes, my initial intel from the Citadel told me the same thing," replied Xavier. "They gathered the scientists to work on creating a virus that they have dubbed 'Tears of the Dragon'."

"Exactly," came the reply. "But what you probably don't know is where they created it. As I've said, I've been analyzing a lot of financial records as well as any and all rumors and mentions of the Brotherhood anywhere on the world wide. What I found was that there is repeated mention of a substance called draculin. It's basically a glycoprotein found in the saliva of vampire bats. It acts as an anticoagulant so that the blood keeps flowing when they put the bite on the victim, so to speak. So based on that I cross-referenced financial transactions from all backers that I could connect with the Brotherhood with areas that would have a plentiful vampire bat population. If you reference the map I've put up on your computer screen you'll see that they leveraged a ton of money into building a state of the art laboratory in Masaya, Nicaragua. It's located at the base of the Masaya volcano on the far side, away from the prying eyes of the city."

Xavier was impressed. "That's incredible Stephen, you've trumped the intelligence that the Citadel had managed to gather by tenfold."

"Of course, but that's not all," came the reply. "Once I knew the location of the lab I tapped into their communication grid. It's all encrypted and I haven't broken it yet but what I do know is that about a week ago there was a ton of communications both in and out of the lab but suddenly about two days ago the whole place went dead, as in stone silent."

Xavier nodded while studying the map, "Thanks Stephen, you've done incredible work. Keep working on the encryption on those communications. We must find out where they are planning to release the virus. In the meantime, I'll head for Masaya."

"No sweat Xavier, I haven't found an encryption yet that I couldn't break. Good luck in Masaya. This is definitely one time that I'm glad

I'm here in my lab instead of out in the field. You can keep the jungle full of vampire bats!"

Approximately thirty four hours later, Xavier found himself in the bustling city of Masaya, Nicaragua. The humid air was stifling compared to the crisp, clean air of the Himalayas and Xavier found himself longing for the cool mountain climate. After settling into his hotel room he rented a jeep and set off for the laboratory. Xavier felt relieved when he got clear of the city and out into the open country. As he rode toward the impressive Masaya volcano Xavier couldn't help but wonder what awaited him at the lab. Had the virus gotten out and killed everyone? Was he walking into a death trap? Would he inadvertently open a sealed door and release a potentially killer virus? There were a lot of questions and not many answers, generally not the way he would like for a case to progress, but he had no choice. Stephen's research had helped them gain some ground, but they were still playing catch up in a game they couldn't afford to lose.

About a mile from the laboratory Xavier pulled the jeep off the side of the dirt road. He would have to make the rest of the trek on foot to keep the element of surprise. He struggled through the undergrowth of the jungle, trying to stay relatively near the road but remain hidden from view. The heat was unbearable, his clothes were soaked to the bone and he found himself fighting an endless barrage of flying insects. Finally he found himself outside of the fence of the laboratory. He stared in at the facility from the bushes and was deeply troubled by what he saw. Inside the fence was a state of the art facility of brick and mortar with a guard station at the front gate, but there appeared to be no guards in the station. Indeed, despite there being several vehicles parked out front, there appeared to be no signs of life. He maneuvered around until he found a spot in the fence that was obstructed from view and pulled a small spray can from his coat pocket. He sprayed it in a circle on the fence and waited as the metal bubbled and melted under the corrosiveness of the acid. He shoved the fence and the circle collapsed in, allowing him to slip through. Xavier worked his way cautiously around the outside of the facility, but his feeling of foreboding grew as he couldn't find a sign of life anywhere. A quick check of the cars showed that they hadn't been driven anytime recently. Xavier approached the door of the facility with a sense of dread. Before opening the door he took a deep breath and found himself almost instinctively putting his sleeve over his mouth, as if that would somehow help. Finally, he pushed the door open and stepped inside the facility.

The cool hiss of air-conditioning swept over him as he stood in the empty lobby. He slowly lowered his arm, wondering if a sudden and horrible death awaited him. Several moments passed and Xavier stood feeling the cold blast of air on his soaking wet skin. He glanced around the lab trying to figure out where everyone had gone. The front security desk was a mess of papers and a full cup of cold coffee sat perched beside a laptop with security camera feeds of the entire complex. Whoever was here, if anyone, definitely knew he was there. Xavier pulled his sword from its hidden scabbard and pushed on through the lab. From the map he had seen at the front desk it looked like the entire facility was a series of small labs built around a larger lab that was located at the back of the facility. As he made his way down the hallways he looked in the windows of the smaller labs and saw notebooks laying on the floor, spilled drinks, and even broken glass. Something had gone seriously wrong. Xavier was beginning to think he may have made a mistake not trying to call in a biohazard team. But that would have taken time, time he didn't have, so he had pushed on alone. For all he knew, he had the virus at this point and it was only a matter of time.

At long last, he reached the main laboratory. He opened the door and walked in to find himself in what was apparently a viewing room, complete with a large window in the center of the wall. Through the window Xavier saw a small man with wild, flowing hair working diligently at gathering books and papers into a big pile in the middle of the floor. It was then that Xavier noticed the rest of the room. All around the man were piles of dead bodies, all stacked neatly against the wall. In all there must have been at least fifteen bodies. Xavier walked over to the door of the laboratory, but thought better of it. Instead, he stowed his katana back under his jacket, moved over directly in front of the window, reached up, and tapped it. The unusual man with the flowing hair stopped suddenly, and jerked his head around to face the window. He stared at the window, at first with fear and then bewilderment. He slowly released the last book onto the pile and moved toward the window, still staring at Xavier. At last they stood mere feet apart with only the window separating them. Slowly the man raised his hand and gave a small wave. Then, with an inquisitive look he reached over to the intercom button and pressed it.

"You're not what I was expecting."

Xavier pressed the button on his side. "I rarely am."

The man smiled. "I was expecting a team of mercenaries with machine guns, you hardly look like a team of mercenaries." Then the man raised his eyebrows, as if gaining some enlightenment. "They didn't send you, did they?"

Xavier narrowed his gaze. "Who are 'they'?"

"The Brotherhood, those zealots. We were brought here under false pretenses with promises of working on a top secret medical advancement. Well you see the progress we've made." The man swept his arm around at the piles of bodies. "This is the fruit of my labor. This, and what may happen to the world if they aren't stopped. You see, I developed a plan to avert the crisis, but lacked the courage to carry it out until it was too late." The man put his arms out and shrugged. "My name is Doctor Vincent Guererro, the man who ended the world." He then let his arms slump to his side and looked around the room.

Xavier started getting the impression that this poor man had cracked under the pressure. He pressed the button on the intercom again. "Vincent, my name is Xavier Greene, I've been sent to stop the Brotherhood from releasing the virus. Any help you can give me would be invaluable."

Vincent shot an icy glare at Xavier. "The virus, that damned virus. 'Tears of the Dragon', they called it. We developed it from the draculin in the bat's saliva. I never knew they planned to release it. If released, it'll spread quickly, and once it matures, it'll be the greatest humanitarian disaster the world has ever seen. And all because I didn't act quickly enough."

Xavier pressed the com button again. "Can you tell me where they plan to release it? I may be able to stop them."

Vincent continued to rant, as if he didn't hear Xavier. "I came up with a plan. Since I was the lead scientist, I was in charge of vaccinations at the lab. It was a simple matter to substitute a slow acting poison for the day's injections. Unfortunately, the day I intended to put my plan into action a group of men showed up and packed up a vial of the virus to take with them. There was nothing I could do. After they left I packed the rest of the virus in a safe in the lab and put my plan into motion anyway. It was the only thing I could do to make up for my transgressions."

Xavier shouted into the intercom, "Vincent! It's not too late! If you help me I can stop them, but I need any information that you can give me!"

Vincent seemed to come out of his rant and ponder the possibility. "Well, maybe you can. It's a long shot though. They mentioned the southeastern United States, it would be a place where a large group of people from all over the world were meeting. Also, you'll find several photographs that I printed from the security camera footage on the desk out there. It has all their faces on it. I know it's not much, but it's all I have. If you do manage to get the virus, it can only be properly destroyed by extremely high heat, so you'll have to find a lab with a very good incinerator."

Xavier replied, "Thank you Vincent. But what about you and the remaining vials of the virus?"

"Oh that's no problem," smiled Vincent. "You see, this lab was built at the base of the volcano for a reason. There is a fail safe that can be activated in the case of an emergency. The wall of the volcano is located directly behind this lab. When it was built, it was lined with explosives. Once detonated, it will cause a breach in the magma chamber and Mother Nature will finish the job. So you better be going Xavier, you'll only have five minutes to get clear, once I press this button." Vincent reached for a button on the console.

"Wait!" shouted Xavier. "My car is about a mile away, I'll never make it in time!"

Vincent's hand paused at the button. "Oh, in that case, there is a set of keys on the desk behind you. It's for the tan Accord parked outside." He watched as Xavier hastily collected the papers and keys. "Good luck Xavier, you're gonna need it. Farewell." Vincent pushed the button and alarms began to sound. Then he turned away from the window and calmly went back to his organizing.

Xavier turned and broke into a dead run through the lab. He burst out the front door and quickly located the Accord. Luckily, it started on the first try, and Xavier spun gravel as he rammed the accelerator to the floor and smashed through the front gate. The car fishtailed and slid all over the loose gravel road, threatening to slip off the road into the underbrush on either side. At last he spotted his Jeep where he had left it and slid the car off the side of the road. He threw his stuff in the jeep, spun it around, and launched it down the narrow road, throwing up a huge dust cloud behind him as he went. The loss of several seconds while changing vehicles was more than made up for by the jeep's superior stability as its tires gripped the rutted, gravel road.

Suddenly, over the roar of the engine, he heard several huge explosions. They erupted from behind him, and he felt a deep rumbling that shook the road and rocked the jeep. In his rearview he saw a cloud of ash and gas boiling up from where the lab was located. He pressed the accelerator to the floor as he was in a deadly race now. He knew if he could make it up the ridge line he would be safe, but the cloud of ash and gas was gaining on him rapidly. When he hit the incline to go up onto the ridge the jeep slid all over the road, twice almost going over the edge. Xavier gritted his teeth and fought to keep the jeep on the road, he didn't dare slow down now. Finally he reached the top of the ridge just as the cloud of gas hit the bottom of the cliff. As he had hoped, it billowed up against the cliff and rose straight up into the sky, it's progress stopped by the natural barrier. At the very top of the ridge, Xavier paused to survey the results of Vincent's handiwork. The valley below was covered in a fog of ash and gas, but in the distance, where the lab was once located, you could see the glow of red hot magma as it flowed freely from the side of the volcano. Now there was only one vial left, and it was up to him to find it.

CHAPTER FIVE

Race Against the Clock

Back at his hotel, Xavier fired up his laptop and sent the coded signal to Stephen that signified he was ready to talk. He then stripped off his ruined suit and took a cold shower. After the shower, he laid out a new suit just as his phone rang and the laptop sprang to life.

"Stephen! What have you found out?"

"Glad to hear the bats didn't get you," came Stephen's reply. "I've managed to crack most of the encryption but it's still just random gibberish and locations."

"Perhaps I can offer some assistance," said Xavier. "I found out that they plan on releasing it in the southeastern United States. Possibly at some sort of gathering."

"Okay, give me a minute." Xavier heard the clicking of keystrokes in the background for a minute or two.

Stephen broke the silence, "I think I have it! The one location on the list that is in the southeast United States is the World Journalism Conference at the WNC Center in downtown Atlanta, Georgia. There's going to be journalists from all over the world at the conference. Anything released there could potentially be carried to the four corners of the Earth."

"Good work Stephen! Can you find a date or time?" replied Xavier.

"I'm working on it. Okay the date I've found is…. Oh shit, you aren't gonna like this. They plan on releasing it in about eight hours."

Xavier quickly did the calculations in his head. "I don't have time to get one of the Citadel's private jets. But maybe I can catch a commercial jet there. I'll need to check the times and if there is one leaving soon, perhaps I can get the Citadel to delay the flight long enough for me to reach the airport."

"No need," replied Stephen. "I've already located a flight out of Nicaragua, it leaves in about twenty minutes and you are about thirty minutes from the airport. Fortunately I've hacked into the computers and set up an hour and a half delay. I'll watch for your ticket to be checked in and remove the delay as soon as you board. By the way, I've loaded some schematics of the WNC Center onto your laptop, I know you prefer to be well researched on your targets!"

Xavier thanked Stephen and logged off. Quickly he got dressed and left for the airport. Once there, he breezed through security. Minutes later, he settled into his seat and opened his laptop to begin studying the schematics. The delay was mysteriously cleared up right after he checked in, and the plane was cleared for take off. The flight was about three and a half hours, so it should give him plenty of time to get there. He checked his watch, just under seven hours to go. He settled in and started going over the schematics as a plan started to form in his head.

Somewhere past Cuba, the captain came over the intercom to announce that due to mechanical problems they were going to have to land in Miami and they would all be switched to another plane, once one could be arranged. Xavier glanced at his watch nervously, they had under four and a half hours until the virus was to be released. This wasn't good.

The plane landed in Miami and Xavier as well as the other passengers were directed to wait until a substitute flight could be found. Xavier turned on his phone and almost immediately got a text to go to Gate F8. At the gate he found a plane that should have left for Atlanta thirty minutes ago, but for some reason had been held up. He gave them his name at the gate and found a reserved ticket waiting for him. Stephen had come through again, like clockwork. Xavier checked his watch as the plane took off, three and a half hours to go.

Three hours and fifteen minutes later the WNC Center was bustling with activity. The World Journalism Conference was in full swing and media personnel from all over the globe had converged on Olympic Park in Atlanta. In all the hustle and bustle of the sea of humanity, Xavier appeared as cool and calm as the rest of the tourists and journalists milling about the food court of the massive WNC Center. Inside however he was on high alert as he actively scanned the crowd, all the while appearing to casually browse the colorful scene in front of him. He adjusted his Fedora, which he had put on in an attempt to block his face from the many security cameras throughout the center.

As he walked the perimeter of the food court he searched the crowd for faces that he had memorized from the security camera footage that Vincent Guererro had provided him. Eventually he recognized a face standing at the second floor balcony. A little further down, he recognized another face and then another, until he realized that there were six members of the Brotherhood around the perimeter of the first and second floors. But who had the virus? It was almost impossible to know. He looked as quickly as he could from person to person, looking for clues, but there was no way to tell. Then he saw him. About twenty feet from Xavier was another member he recognized from the photos. The man's face was familiar, but what was more important was the amount of sweat on the man's face. While he walked normally enough, not rushed or awkward, his face was awash with the stress that would come from being the man who had to pull the trigger on the end of the world.

Slowly, the man walked to the dead center of the busy food court. Once there he calmly removed a small vial from a bag he was carrying under his arm. He paused just a second, as if saying a prayer and extended his arm out to his side, vial in hand. He stood for a few short seconds, as if contemplating what he was about to do. Finally, he opened his hand and let the vial fall, awaiting the sound of the breaking glass that would signify the end of the mission, as well as his life. He waited an eternity for the sound, but it never came. Suddenly his earpiece erupted into a sea of cacophony.

"He grabbed it! Who the hell is that??" exclaimed the voices in his ear. Startled, he looked up to see a man in a black suit and fedora moving away from him at a casual, but quick pace.

On the second floor balcony, Marcus Jamali couldn't believe what he was seeing. Just as the vial was being dropped, a figure had come out of nowhere and just nonchalantly snatched it out of midair. The figure was so quick that he was almost 20 feet away before anyone could process what had just happened. Marcus's eyes followed him as he appeared to be making his way toward the men's bathroom on the far side.

"Somebody grab him! He's heading east!" barked Marcus into his earpiece.

About the time Xavier reached the bathroom door, a member of the Brotherhood approached, pulling a gun from beneath his jacket. 'Perfect', thought Xavier. Just as the figure reached him, he deflected the gun out of the man's hand and slipped behind him. Grabbing the man's neck, he wrenched it at an impossible angle, cracking the vertebrae. The man dropped to the floor, as startled journalists jumped back out of the way. Xavier then casually scooped up the man's gun and fired it straight up into the air. The effect was immediate. Whereas a few people had been curious about the altercation, there was now a straight up stampede of people desperately trying to vacate the premises. Xavier moved quickly to the bathroom door, pausing to make sure the Brotherhood saw him before disappearing into the doorway.

Marcus and the other brotherhood members assembled on the first level near the bathroom. Discreetly, they all pulled their weapons, and while holding them under their jackets, they approached the bathroom. Just as they reached the doorway, there was a flash and a cloud of smoke began to billow out from the bathroom. Marcus held them off, not wanting to push forward into a potential trap, but they couldn't wait much longer. There was a full scale stampede going on around them and if they stayed in the open too long, they were gonna attract the attention of the police. Finally, he decided they could wait no longer and charged into the bathroom, only to find the room completely deserted. Marcus and the rest of his team put their guns away under their coats and rushed back out of the bathroom. Looking around in the sea of people they could see no signs of him. He had vanished like a ghost, and taken the virus with him.

Next door to the bathroom at Josie's Organic Burgers, the employees were crowded around the front counter watching the chaos explode in front of them.

"Should we close the gate?" asked Andy, looking at shift manager Brian.

"Are you kidding?" replied Brian. "George will have our hide if we close early. I don't care what's going on, until the cops tell us to get out, we stay. It ain't worth the ass chewing we'll get."

Andy nodded his head in agreement, George's temper tantrums were notorious. What neither noticed was the ceiling tile that lifted up, and the figure that dropped down in the back of the restaurant. Xavier walked to the backdoor of the kitchen, dropped his fedora in the trash can, and exited out of the chaos into the humid, Georgia afternoon heat. Once outside, Xavier paused just long enough to place the vial in a padded case, which he placed in the inside pocket of his jacket. Then he turned, and slipped through the crowd across Olympic Park.

CHAPTER SIX

A Brief Respite

The Citadel operates a "shadow world" in the plain view of the normal one. Hidden among normal houses and businesses are Citadel facilities that work as safe houses. It was at one of these facilities that Xavier now found himself sitting comfortably on an oversized sofa, sipping green tea that the attendant had brought him. Each "safe house" location had a full staff of attendants that would assist an agent in any way possible, as well as clean up and cook for them. Xavier sat and waited on his dinner, pondering how far this air conditioned urban living was from the extremes of Tibet and the humid heat of Nicaragua. For the first time since this mission had started, he had taken the time to take a deep breath and ease the tension that he had been carrying since Lhasa. The attendant came by again to let Xavier know that his meal would be ready in approximately thirty minutes. Xavier figured this was as good a time as any to report in to David, so he made his way to the secure line used to call in and report.

The phone rang several times before David picked up. "This is David."

"Hello David, it's Xavier. It's done."

"Really? Excellent news! I see from the phone you are calling from that you are in Atlanta. You've covered quite a bit of ground, old man! So, you have the virus?" asked David.

Xavier proceeded to fill him in on an outline of the details of the mission, telling him about Masaya and the tragic tale of Vincent Guererro, the flight to Atlanta, and finally the chaos at the WNC Center.

David replied. "So that was you. I saw the news about a disturbance at the WNC Center and wondered if you had anything to do with it. So I am to understand that you have it in your possession?"

Xavier replied, "Yes, I have it with me now and it's secure. Now I just need orders on where to take it to dispose of it. The late Dr. Guererro told me that it takes a high level incinerator to destroy the virus completely. I trust you can provide me with such a facility?"

"Without a doubt," replied David. "I'll report on your progress and get further orders. Have you made arrangements with the garage?"

The garage was another service provided by the Citadel, allowing it's agents to contact it and obtain transportation. Xavier had put in a call right after he arrived at the safe house.

"I'm supposed to go there first thing in the morning and pick up a car. I called them earlier." Xavier replied as rubbed his temple. He could feel a slight aching, perhaps he needed the rest more than he realized.

David replied, "Good, get yourself a good night's rest and call me when you reach the garage tomorrow. I should have further instructions then. Good night Xavier."

"Good night David." Xavier hung up the phone and rubbed his eyes. The dull throb continued in his temple as he drained his tea. He then got up and wandered toward the dining room for what would no doubt be an exceptional meal. The only thing he looked forward to more than the warm meal was the full night's sleep he would get afterwards. He looked forward to putting this mission to rest and returning home.

***

Across town, Marcus Jamali was ranting into the phone. "Who the hell was that? How could that have happened? You told us you had it all worked out."

"Please Marcus, calm down." The voice on the other side of the phone was unusually cold and calm.

"I have reviewed the footage and I'm still gathering data, but I can tell you that he was definitely a pro. I have a shot of his face that should allow us to run facial recognition. We'll find him, trust me, I have eyes everywhere."

Marcus paced the floor. He didn't like this situation at all. He didn't doubt the skill of the hacker on the other end of the phone but he also didn't like the feeling that this whole situation was spiraling out of his control. Several years ago a mysterious backer had approached the Brotherhood with a ton of money, and a powerful hacker on their side. They promised big things for the Brotherhood, a chance at legitimacy. The Brotherhood had accepted the offer and started following the direction of this powerful, mysterious entity. Then their benefactor had made his master plan clear. The world needed purging and the Brotherhood, with his help, would be the catalyst and 'Tears of the Dragon' would be their weapon. With it they would cleanse the world of the greed and corruption that had run rampant. It was a chance for the Brotherhood to take a stand and mean something. Marcus took great pride in that, but at the same time, it was also further than they had ever taken the Brotherhood and at times he felt in over his head.

The voice on the phone came back, "Okay I've run the security footage and managed to get enough of a hit to run my program versus the traffic cameras in the area. I've found our friend and tracked him across town to an approximate area. I forwarded the coordinates to your laptop. I also ran him through facial recognition software."

Marcus finally replied, "Well, are you gonna tell us or what? Who is he, where is he, and when do we get to take back what is ours?"

The voice replied with almost an air of annoyance, "Well that's the thing. I came up with nothing. Our friend doesn't technically exist. He's a ghost, there is literally no record of him anywhere. Furthermore, while I've been unable to find his identity, I have found a match to his picture. He seems to always show up at big events, such as revolutions, change of regime, high pressure situations. This would tell me that this is no ordinary thief you are dealing with. Since that's the case, I have to advise you to proceed with extreme caution. In the meantime I will do more research and try to find his true identity."

The phone clicked dead. Marcus tossed it down on the desk and paced the room. As if he wasn't already apprehensive about this whole thing, now they had the problem of their mystery thief. Marcus sat down and drained his glass of bourbon. He didn't care how dangerous this mystery person might be, he was just one person and if he knew anything, it was how to take care of a thief. He looked at the coordinates on his laptop and smiled. Tomorrow he would make him pay, too much planning had gone into this to let this interloper ruin it all. Tomorrow his luck would run out, Marcus would make sure of it.

CHAPTER SEVEN

A Troubling Vision

The meal had been as good as he hoped it would be. The exact polar opposite of the bland porridge at the monastery. But even as good as it was, Xavier had trouble enjoying it. The throbbing in his temples that had started earlier that evening had continued and grew in intensity. After dinner, he had retired to his room and meditated until it had mostly subsided. Then, after taking a shower, he laid down and fell into a deep slumber.

Deep in his subconscious, Xavier dreamed of walking a quiet, dark street, the buildings all strangely lit by the glow on the horizon. Large flakes of snow fell slowly around him. Xavier walked in just his suit, oblivious to the cold. He thought about how it reminded him of his time in Moscow a few years ago.

Just ahead, there was movement in the snow. He moved in for a closer look and saw a small creature wriggling in the snow. Slowly, like when he was a child, he scooped up the creature. After blowing away the curiously dry snow from the creature, he saw it for what it was. In his hand was a small, Chinese Dragon. It's petite, slender, serpentine body writhed in his hand as it's long claws pawed, trying to find a place to grasp onto. Its head, far too large for its body with a mane and horns protruding out of it, snapped and hissed at him. He smiled at the tiny creature, it reminded him of toys he had when he was a child. Tenderly he took the creature by its tail and put it into the chest pocket of his jacket. It struggled mightily against his efforts but he forced the small creature in. It continued to struggle, and he buttoned the pocket, just to make sure the small dragon was secure.

As he continued to walk down the sidewalk, he looked at the

buildings lining both sides of the road. As he continued, he started to notice that the buildings, while brightly lit from the glow in the distance, were all black and charred, as if from a fire. He looked around puzzled, as if just realizing something. He put his hand out and caught a snowflake in it. He rubbed it between his fingers and found that it crumbled to dust and smudged on his skin. It was then that he realized it wasn't snow at all. What was falling all around him was ash. The buildings were black because they had burnt and he started to have a sinking feeling he knew where the glow lighting everything around him was coming from. Just then, an intense, sharp pain struck him in the chest and drove him to his knees. He convulsed against the pain, feeling as though his rib cage was going to explode outward. The pain intensified until he could barely think, and suddenly a huge dragon erupted from his chest. He screamed in agony and collapsed backwards as the huge beast curled around itself in the sky just above him. The face had grown more distorted, the horns larger, the mane longer. It was a magnificent creature, spiraling above his barely conscious form. But he also felt a malignant evil in it, a void that could not, would not be satisfied until it had devoured the entire world.

The creature continued to spiral for a few more moments before it turned its attention to Xavier. With one quick motion, it swept Xavier up in its claw and held him. He tried to struggle but found his arms felt like lead, he was helpless. The creature opened it's great mouth to swallow him up, lifting him with it's claw, its eyes gleaming with a malevolent glee. Just before it threw him into its gaping jaws, Xavier looked it directly in the eye and saw that instead of pupils the dragon's eyes each contained the planet Earth, blazing with fire. Xavier glanced back over his shoulder and saw that the glow around them was the world burning. He turned back to see the dragon roar before throwing him into its chasm of a mouth. He fell screaming into the blackness.

Xavier bolted upright in his bed, his face glistening with sweat. Slowly he got his breathing under control and ran a hand through his soaking hair. He glanced over at the padded case, sitting on his nightstand. He could still hear the roar of the dragon, feel the heat of his breath. Worst of all, he could still smell the burning structures and flesh. He reached over and slowly patted the case, as if to reassure himself that it was just a dream. With a troubled mind, he slowly relaxed and tried to ease himself into a sleep that would not come.

CHAPTER EIGHT

Nowhere to Run To

Xavier left for the garage early the next morning. He had disguised himself in an oversized tracksuit with a dirty hoodie pulled over the top. He carried his duffle bag over his shoulder and slumped as he seemed to wander aimlessly through the city. For all appearances he was one of the many homeless people that call Atlanta home. The city's homeless are myriad but invisible. The business men and women who walk the busy sidewalks of Atlanta are in too much of a hurry running to and from meetings to ever notice them. Twice Xavier thought he saw members of the Brotherhood drive by in black SUVs. He wondered how they could possibly have any idea where he went. That, coupled with the strange dream he had the night before, had brought back the tension in his temple. But there was also a growing feeling of suspicion inside him. Something didn't feel right. The Brotherhood had always been a small time organization but in the last two years they had grown incredibly organized and definitely had someone bankrolling them, but who? And how did they know his approximate location? It couldn't have been a coincidence that they just happened to be in the area where he was traveling. Atlanta was too big of a city for that kind of happenstance.

Xavier slipped into the side door of a fast food restaurant with a "Free Wifi" sign in the window. He sat down in a booth in the back, pulled out his laptop, and fired it up. As he did, he noticed two other homeless people had followed his lead and we're now huddling in a corner booth on the opposite end of the room. Once he was online, he immediately constructed an encrypted message to Stephen, asking him to look further into the financial backing of the Brotherhood and also, just as a precaution, to look up any abandoned biotech labs that would have an incinerator that fit his need. Xavier almost deleted the part about the biotech lab, feeling foolish for doubting the Citadel. They had never let him down before, but Xavier feared the allure of the power that the virus held. Whoever had the virus could hold the world hostage and nothing was more seductive and corrupting than the promise of power. Just as he finished sending the email and was powering down his laptop, a security guard came around the corner.

"What the- oh hell no! You know we don't allow your kind in here," said the guard as he approached the two homeless people in the corner booth. "Get out of here and find another place to squat!"

He raised his arm as if threatening to strike them, and they tripped over one another trying to get out of the booth. Just then he noticed Xavier, who was busy stashing his laptop away.

"And wait just a minute, what do you think you're doing?" said the guard as he approached Xavier.

Xavier had packed up the laptop, grabbed his bag, and slid out of the booth, trying to slip by without a scene, but the guard grabbed the strap on his duffle bag as he attempted to pass him.

"Oh no you don't. I saw that computer, where'd you get something like that? Did somebody leave their window down on their car? You just sit back down until the cops get here." He pushed Xavier back toward the booth as he reached for his radio. Suddenly, Xavier twisted the guard's wrist, while pivoting his weight and the guard tumbled into the seat of the booth. Simultaneously his fist darted out and connected with a pressure point at the base of the guard's skull, rendering him unconscious. Xavier gently slumped the guard forward and placed his head on his crossed arms, as if taking a nap. He then picked up the guard's hat and sat it on the table next to him. He turned to leave and saw the two homeless men watching him with wide eyes. Xavier placed a finger to his lips, and shook his head side to side slowly. The men nodded and slipped out the door. Once outside, Xavier reached into his duffle bag and pulled out a container of food from the safe house that he had taken with him for the road. He called to the two men and handed them the food. They still stared at Xavier with wide eyes, as if trying to figure out who or what he was. One of them managed to say a thank you before Xavier turned and set off back down the street toward the garage.

Approximately thirty minutes later, Xavier arrived at the garage and was greeted by George Thomas, the head mechanic. He informed him that he could have his pick of any of the cars in the garage, and left to get his paperwork while he chose. Xavier walked down the rows of cars, amazed at the vast array of Ferrari, BMW, Mercedes, SUV and other audacious rides. Xavier shook his head wondering why they bothered with all these glamorous toys. To blend in you would need something that people wouldn't notice, not a flashy sports car, like some secret agent from the sixties. He continued milling through until he saw something that fit the bill. Just then George arrived with the paperwork.

"Have you made your choice?" The mechanic asked.

"Indeed, I have," replied Xavier. "I'll take that one." He pointed back to the corner where an old, brown Pinto sat. Its body was splattered with rust spots and chips in the paint.

George let out a short chuckle. "Now that's an odd request! Are you serious? Why would you want that little rust bucket?"

Xavier smiled at the mechanic. "I believe you just answered that question for yourself. If you saw this car out on the road would you even notice it?"

The mechanic slowly nodded his head while staring at the car. "Well you know that's not an official vehicle. This car actually belonged to one of my workers. He gave it to me and I've been working on it in my spare time as a practice project. It has a gps system behind the dash, but not nearly as many bells and whistles as the others."

"Believe me, that will do," replied Xavier. "All that I require is that it runs. And if you don't mind, there are a few small modifications that would assist me. Nothing that should take any time. Will it need any additional modifications to make it drivable?"

George glanced back at Xavier. "Oh trust me, it's roadworthy. I've completely overhauled the engine. It gets pretty killer gas mileage as well. What modifications do you have in mind?"

"I need hidden storage in the hatchback of the car for my gear and my cargo. Nothing elaborate, just efficient and safe. The space for the cargo will need extra padding."

George pulled out a pad and sketched up a rough outline of the trunk and showed it to Xavier. "Something like this?"

"Yes, exactly," came Xavier's reply. "Now where do you keep your secure line?"

Moments later Xavier had changed back into his suit and was sitting in a back office of the garage waiting on David to pick up. Normally he picked up on the second ring but as the phone reached it's sixth ring, he was beginning to worry. At that moment he heard the phone click and David picked up.

"Ah David, you had me worried." Then he heard the unsteadiness in David's voice.

"Xavier, yes, sorry for the delay. Um, I don't know how to put this, except to tell you there has been a change of plans." David's voice wavered on the last few words.

Xavier paused and let the silence stretch out before replying. "I see. What are the new orders?" Even though he was already sure what the answer would be.

David also paused slightly before continuing, as if carefully thinking out his response. "Well, I filed your report last night and it was well received. I was told they would find a facility and give me a location this morning. But when the call came in today the orders had been amended. According to the new orders, you are to immediately take the virus to a safe house location in upstate New York and turn it over to an agent you will meet there."

Xavier sat holding the phone, half shocked. His hunch had come true. But he had never seen the Citadel make such a self serving move before. As he contemplated his next words, David started speaking again.

"By the way, sorry for letting the phone ring so long. I'm afraid I'm experiencing some technical glitches. It's interfering with our phone security. I'm afraid this call isn't being monitored or recorded, as would be the normal protocol." He let the words sink in. "So the only people who know about this conversation are you and I."

Realizing he was free to speak, Xavier snapped out of his thoughts. "David, what in the hell is going on? This can't be a legit order!"

"Oh it's a legit order." Replied David. "However it's highly unusual, which is why I found it a convenient time to have a security lapse so that we could speak freely. You see, the Citadel has everything broken down into different 'stations'. That way if there is ever a security breach then everything is compartmentalized, and it lessens the amount of secrets that a saboteur can get their hands on. That way, no one knows everything. Well the orders normally all come through the exact same station, except this morning the change of orders came from a different station. I thought that was odd, until I looked up the safe house where they wanted you to take the package. It's run by the exact same station that sent me the orders. I'm also under strict orders to only report to them on this case from here on out."

Xavier pondered what David had said. "This is all very troubling David. This whole thing smells of some sort of scheme. You don't think that this other 'station' is trying to use the virus in some sort of power play do you? From my understanding, the Citadel has always worked because the power of all the members remained balanced and fair. Something like this virus would cause a major tipping of the scales, so to speak. No organization or country could be trusted with that kind of power."

"However," interjected David. "I have to point out that as unusual as the circumstances are, it isn't our place to question them. We must follow the chain of command, no matter our personal feelings. There are strict policies about the handling of agents who don't follow orders."

Xavier let the silence drag out as he pondered the situation he had found himself in. On one hand, he knew he had his orders, but on the other hand, he had the promise that he made to Quan-Li to protect the innocent. If he let the virus pass through his hands, he would be endangering the human race and untold innocent people could die. To disobey a direct order most certainly meant his own death, but what if it was just one faction trying to make a power play as he suspected? Xavier made up his mind, to him there was no other logical solution.

"David, I'm sorry but I can't bring the virus to the safe house," replied Xavier.

"I'm I to assume that you are going 'rogue'?" asked David, shocked by Xavier's statement.

"No, not at all," replied Xavier. "I'm merely following the original parameters of my mission, which is to destroy the virus. Based on the fact that the orders didn't come through the normal channels, I'm going to disregard the new orders and continue with my mission."

David replied in a shaky, rattled voice. "You know there will most certainly be consequences. Even if this is a faction acting on it's own self interest within the Citadel, they will retaliate and try to claim the virus themselves."

"I'm aware that it's a huge gamble, but hopefully my insubordination will help draw attention to what's really going on. In any case, it will at least buy some time, so that hopefully the rest of the Citadel will figure out what is going on," said Xavier as a plan started to form in the back of his mind.

"Well, if you've made up your mind, then that's that," replied David. "But it's a huge gamble that has a high probability of you winding up dead. Also, from here on out I will be unable to provide you with assistance."

"Indeed," nodded Xavier. "But if I do nothing and follow orders we could all end up dead anyway. I have an associate working on a suitable place to destroy the virus. Once I hear from him I will proceed with the disposal. Once I dispose of it, I'll call you to report, assuming I'm still alive. In the meantime I have a favor to ask of you."

"And just what is that?" asked David.

"I need you to delay your report at least until I get away from the garage. I need all the head start I can get."

David paused a few seconds before replying. "Well I am obligated to report your intent, however I can't do anything about the fact that I'm having technical difficulties with my equipment. I won't be able to stall for long as the system has an annoying habit of resetting itself before too long, but I'll do what I can."

"Thank you David, I appreciate it. Hopefully I'll be back in touch in a few days," replied Xavier.

"You're welcome. Good luck and Godspeed. You'll need it." The phone clicked off.

Xavier immediately opened his laptop to check for a message from Stephen. He had one message from Stephen, informing him that he would continue his inquiry into the financing of the Brotherhood. In the meantime he had found a recently decommissioned government lab in the Southwestern United States. It's a state of the art laboratory that had been deactivated due to budget cuts. It definitely had the hardware to deal with the virus. It would however take a few days to get the credentials together, after which he would be in touch. Stephen then provided Xavier with the coordinates of the lab. Xavier copied them onto a notepad, and powered his computer off. He would have to move quickly to get away from the garage before David submitted his report.

In the main bay of the garage, George was just putting the finishing touches on the modifications. It was a great piece of work for a rush job. No one would suspect that the hatch of the Pinto contained no less than six secret compartments, built to Xavier's specifications. Just then, Xavier approached the car at a brisk pace.

"Ah there you are!" Said George, opening the trunk so Xavier could see. "I just got it finished up, isn't it a beauty?"

Xavier opened the main panel and stowed his duffle bag, much to George's annoyance. "Indeed it is! There see? The bag fits like a glove!"

Xavier then began to stuff his other belongings into the other compartments.

"What's the rush?" asked George, as he dodged out of Xavier's way.

"Change of plans," replied Xavier. "My timeline has been moved up drastically. I'm going to be lucky if I can reach my destination in time."

"Well yeah, I understand that. But this isn't a regulation car, I haven't even installed the required tracking chip yet," replied George, turning to his table. "All I have to do is calibrate it and then it'll take me about twenty minutes to install." Xavier couldn't believe his luck. By picking a car that wasn't in the fleet, he may have bought himself an opening.

"No, I don't have time," sputtered Xavier, showing a frustration that was only part manufactured. "If I don't make this deadline, heads will roll. You don't want them coming down on you for holding up the operation do you?"

George shrugged his shoulders. "Fine, I've set it up to calibrate. Just throw it in the backseat for now. Have somebody fasten it for you when you reach your destination." He tossed Xavier the device, which he then tossed into the back floorboard. Xavier got in the drivers seat and adjusted it to be as comfortable as you could get in a Pinto. Just then he saw George come running back up to the car.

"Hey!" yelled George.

Xavier tried to hide his surprise. "Yes?"

"You forgot the keys. Don't know how you planned to get their otherwise." He tossed the keys in the window.

"Thanks!" said Xavier as he started the car and sped out of the garage.

Several blocks away Xavier pulled into an alleyway and got out of the car. Going around to the back, he finished arranging his belongings that he had haphazardly thrown in earlier. When he had emptied a small travel bag, he went around to the backseat and retrieved the tracking device. It was almost finished calibrating and once it was online it would broadcast his whereabouts to the Citadel. If that happened, he would be lucky if he made it out of the city. He placed the device in a bag and walked around the corner. He had picked this alleyway because he had seen a Greyhound bus loading out behind a hotel. Beside the bus, a large stack of luggage sat waiting to be loaded. As he walked by, Xavier nonchalantly dropped the bag into the pile of luggage and returned to his car. He then removed the case containing the virus from his jacket and put it in the special padded compartment that George had made for him. Once it was secure, he went back around to the driver's seat, settled in and started the car. He checked the coordinates and found that the lab Stephen found for him was in Arizona. It was a long drive, but he remembered George bragging to him about the modifications to the engine and the improved gas mileage. This car would do. Just as he started to settle in, Xavier glanced at the back of the car and thought about the deadly cargo contained therein. Arizona couldn't come soon enough.

CHAPTER NINE

By the Time I Get to Arizona...

In a darkened room, lit only by computer screens, a figure hunched over his keyboard. The only sounds were the clicks of his fingers on the keys and the hum of server fans. Beside the keyboard was an ever growing pile of pistachio shells. His hand reached over and fumbled for another pistachio, when suddenly an alert pinged on one of his myriad screens. He adjusted his glasses and stared at the grainy picture of the mysterious figure walking into a convenience store. Subconsciously he cracked a pistachio shell with his teeth and spit it into the pile. He watched for a few more seconds and grinned. He had found him at last. It was unusual for someone to elude him this long.

He had hacked into the Citadel's tracking device and thought he had him dead to rights, only to find that he had sent Marcus on a wild goose chase. It was embarrassing, but only a minor setback. He had bragged to Marcus that he had eyes everywhere and he did. He watched as the figure left the store and switched to the parking lot camera to continue the surveillance. The man got into his car and he quickly clicked a screenshot of the license plate. A large grin spread across his face as he picked up the phone to call Marcus. This annoying man may have a head start but he also has no idea he is being pursued and now that he had the make, model, and license plate, he could track him anywhere.

***

The drive to Arizona was approximately twenty seven hours and even though it was low key and inconspicuous, the Pinto that Xavier had picked wasn't the most comfortable car. He had driven all day and into the night, from Alabama, through the plains of Oklahoma, the panhandle of Texas, and past the mesa's of New Mexico. Now as he entered Arizona his legs and lower back were aching and he really needed a good stretch. He thought about pulling over long enough to stretch them out for a few minutes, but something in the rearview caught his eye. Out in the distance behind him, he saw a black SUV, and it appeared to be gaining on him. He wondered if the heat and exhaustion were getting to him. It had been an extremely long drive, and even he had his limits. There was also the ever present thought of the terrible cargo that lay just behind the backseat of the Pinto. He had been thinking of that a lot during the drive and caught himself staring at the spot where it laid many times. He thought about the families on vacation that he had passed on the highway. Oblivious to the fact that certain death was passing right by them in the unassuming car that the kids probably made fun of as it passed. He glanced up in the rear view and noticed that the SUV was definitely gaining on him now. He decided that some evasive action was warranted, even if he was being paranoid. Besides it would help snap him out of the lull of the long drive. Now he just needed to come up with a plan.

He didn't have to wait long for a plan to come together. As they neared the exit for Highway 191 an eighteen wheeler moved into the middle lane, obscuring the view of the SUV. When it did Xavier slowed his car so he could keep the SUV on the other side of the large truck and got ready to make his move. Just as the SUV made its move to the left to pass the tractor-trailer, Xavier slammed on brakes, slid into the right lane and exited onto 191. The SUV sped by the exit and continued down the highway. Xavier merged onto 191 and continued south for a quarter mile, pushing the small engine as hard as he could, before jumping off on Indian Route 9402 and driving through the small town of Sanders. He weaved his way through the backroads of the town until he came back out further south on 191. From there he decided he would take some country roads and meet back up with Highway 40 a bit further west, just to be safe. Xavier caught himself once again glancing back at the hidden compartment where the virus laid in wait. He rubbed his eyes and thought about how glad he would be when this was over. He still questioned why he had allowed himself to be freaked out and abandon his route. The chances that the SUV he had seen on the highway belonged to the Brotherhood were slim to none and he knew it. Yet he diverted his route and lost precious time because of it. He rolled his shoulders to try to alleviate some of the tension in his neck as he navigated the backroads. He knew it was the added stress of having the virus with him. The pressure he felt carrying his deadly cargo added to the fatigue and exhaustion that were setting in, he knew if he didn't get rest soon he would be in dire straits.

***

"What do you mean you can't find him?" Marcus Jamali yelled into his phone. This long pursuit across the country was taking its toll on him as well and he wasn't amused that their target had once again given them the slip.

"You have to understand when you get out in the Southwest, away from the population centers, there are less cameras, it's simply harder to track him," the voice on the phone replied. He had orders to help Marcus, however the impatience and arrogance that he got in return was making it difficult, even for a patient person such as himself. "Keep calm and stay on the highway. He will turn up sooner or later and I'll notify you as soon as I find him."

Marcus heard the click and the phone went dead. He wished he could reach through the phone and strangle the smug bastard on the other end. The last couple days had been one fiasco after another. First they ended up tailing a Greyhound on a wild goose chase in Atlanta, then to make matters worse, somewhere back in Texas the air-conditioning had went out on the truck. Now, just when they were closing in on the quarry, he gave them the slip, and once again disappeared into thin air. Marcus knew one thing, when he caught up with this mystery person, he was definitely gonna give him some serious payback.

***

Xavier finally decided to stop in the town of Wingfield, Arizona. The tiny, little town sat just off the historic Route 66 and made a staggering amount of it's money off of tourism. It was also about forty five minutes to the southeast of his destination, the Hastings BioTech Facility. Xavier cruised through the streets until he spotted a cafe with Wifi and parked out back. He logged on to their network and fired up his encryption program. A few minutes later, he received a message from Stephen explaining that they would have to wait a few more days to get into the lab as he was having trouble securing the credentials. The lab was only recently shut down, and it's servers were still being maintained by the government. Currently they were undergoing routine maintenance and Stephen couldn't do anything until that was completed. Xavier stared in the rearview at the compartment in the back of the Pinto. This wasn't good, he needed to get rid of the virus as soon as possible. Every delay increased the chance that other players would get involved. He sighed heavily. There was nothing he could do at this point. He stretched his fingers and set about bringing up a map of Wingfield. At first glance it was your typical Southwestern tourist town but after some studying he found that it had a sewer system, one of the few small towns in the southwest that did. He made a mental note, since that bit of knowledge could come in handy. Scouring the map for a little longer he found an area of town that fit his needs; a mostly rundown, abandoned warehouse district.

An hour later, Xavier picked the lock on a four story building in the warehouse district and slipped inside. Pulling a flashlight from his duffle bag, he worked his way through the dusty, old offices up to the third floor. Once there, he selected what appeared to be an old tax office in the middle of the building and began setting up shop. First, he hid the padded case carrying the virus in a secure location. Then he pulled several small devices and a small key fob from his bag. Heading back downstairs, he went around and placed a device at every door, checking them as he went. The devices were motion sensors that when triggered would cause the key fob to vibrate in Xavier's pocket. After testing them all and double-checking the exits, Xavier returned to the office on the third floor. He reached in his bag and pulled out a small, thin rolled up pad. After removing his jacket and tie, he laid down on the pad and started working through releasing the considerable tension that had built up in his body. After a few moments, the exhaustion of the past few days came rushing in on him and he fell deep asleep.

CHAPTER TEN

Pressure Dream

In his dream, he was terrified and running through the ruins. He ran as fast as he could, legs burning from the effort. Finally he collapsed behind a broken wall, gasping from the effort. Doubled over, his chest heaved from not being able to catch his breath. When at once a rumbling started, first as a subtle vibration, then building into an ominous, low growl. The ground trembled when finally, the terrible thing rolled into view. It's scales were as perfect as the finest ivory, it's huge mane like silk, it's eyes two glowing orbs set into a ghastly face. It's claws scratched across the buildings as it rumbled through the ruins. It's terrible head swiveled side to side, sniffing the air as it went, looking here and there, searching for its prey.

Xavier could feel it behind the wall, he could feel the heat of it's breath, the smell of burning flesh. Suddenly, he could take it no longer and burst from his hiding spot, running for his life from this hideous beast. Instantly, the dragon saw him and roared as it gave chase. Xavier ran as hard as he could, but still felt the dragon almost nipping at his heels. Just when it seemed it would catch him, the ground gave way and he fell into a huge pit. He crashed into a sea of debris and laid there, waiting for the dragon to finish him. But to his surprise, it never came. Xavier laid as still as he could, not daring to move for fear that the dragon would come back and finish him off. When he hadn't seen or heard it for several minutes, he decided he needed to get up and find cover. Struggling against the debris under him, he sat up and quickly came to the realization that what he had landed on wasn't a pile of rubble at all. He looked around and as far as he could see, the entire pit was full of human bones. Xavier tried to jump to his feet but quickly lost his footing in the shifting pile of bones. In fact, the more he struggled, the more the bones shifted, not allowing him any foot hold. As he continued to struggle, the bones began to change, starting around the edges of the pit at first, but slowly working it's way in toward him. The bones all slowly dissolved into a thick, white liquid, the consistency of a bog. Xavier worked furiously to free himself from the wretched substance. He struggled and swam to the edge of it, if only he could reach the wall! But, as he reached the edge and started trying to find a handhold to climb up and out, skeletal arms shot out of the liquid and grabbed Xavier. The arms pulled him away from the wall and back into the sludge. He fought as hard as he could, but it was no use, there were too many arms, as even more came up to pull and scratch at him. As the struggle continued, he felt his head go under and the horrible, wretched substance filled his nose, mouth and lungs. It was a sensation not unlike drowning in porridge.

Xavier jolted awake into a seated position on the mat he had spread on the floor. He sat in the dark for several minutes, breathing heavily, trying to will himself back to reality. Eventually, he began to slow his breathing and calm his mind. His body was soaking wet from the cold sweat he had broken out in during the dream. He shivered uncontrollably, but slowly his breathing returned to a normal rhythm and quieted his nerves. He switched on a small lamp that he had found on a shelf in the office and walked over to where the virus was hidden. It was obvious to him that the presence of the virus and the pressure of having it in his possession were having an effect on him, but what choice did he have? The lack of sleep and the fatigue caused by the near constant travel hadn't helped the matter. He reached and opened the loose floorboard where he had the virus hidden. There was the padded case, still sitting exactly where he left it. Slowly he lifted the case out of the space on the floor and opened it. With a slight hesitation, he removed the vial containing the virus from the case and held it up to the light. It was completely remarkable to him that something so small could potentially cause so much destruction and death. He also thought about the growing problem with the Citadel, and how his orders had been abruptly changed. Now he was out on his own, improvising a plan to destroy the virus, with no backup. He thought about the Brotherhood and their righteous crusade. As misguided as it was, he did understand their point of view. Over the years, the world had become corrupt, from the greed and excess that was constantly broadcast on tv, to the governments and corporations that secretly controlled them. Everyone seemed to only be out for themselves, at the expense of everyone else. Those in power hoarded money and resources, at the expense of the most vulnerable. It was true that all it would take was a turn of the lid on the vial and that corruption could be eradicated, purged from the Earth. But at what cost? He thought of the homeless people in Atlanta, the innocent families he passed on the highways, he even thought of Quan-Li, who had saved him when everyone else had abandoned him. No, there were good people in the world, good people worth saving. Even in the darkest times, you had to have faith in the goodness of mankind. You had to have hope, for hope was a powerful weapon, one that could light the darkness of despair.

It was at this moment that he realized he had been absentmindedly rubbing his finger against the lid of the vial. He checked the seal to make sure it hadn't been disturbed, slid it back into the padded case, and returned it to it's hiding place. Returning to his mat, he sat and pondered the situation. He realized that the Brotherhood thought their mission was righteous, and would do anything to complete it. But he also realized from his time with Quan-Li, that no matter how horrible the world could be, and how corrupt some people are, it was no one's place to decide when the world ends. Not his, not the Brotherhood's. In the end there is balance, and as long as the virus exists, that balance is threatened. Xavier knew it was up to him to restore that balance, it was his burden to bear. He had to endure, no matter what. He had no help, no allies and the longer it stretched on, the lower his odds, but he would find a way to succeed, no matter what. With a renewed focus, Xavier turned out the lamp and lay back on the mat again. Meditating and calming himself, he started over with his exercise of releasing the stress from his body until he once again fell asleep.

CHAPTER ELEVEN

Early Morning Ambush

The early morning sun cast long shadows across the arid Arizona landscape as a single figure walked back down the road toward town. After dozing on and off for several hours, Xavier had decided it was a lost cause to try to pursue the sleep that had proven so elusive. Instead, he decided to turn his attention towards his own hygiene, which had been painfully neglected during the last few days. If he had no choice but to wait here, he might as well put the time to good use. He had remembered passing a truck stop and had walked the half mile up the road to take a much needed shower and change into fresh clothes.

As he walked back down the dusty road toward the warehouses his stomach groaned. He rubbed it absentmindedly and thought about the fact he had basically been living off of gas station food and beef jerky for the last week. After a quick stop by the warehouse to make sure the safeguards were still in place, Xavier set out walking the short distance into downtown to eat at a small cafe he had seen on the main strip.

The main strip of town held a wide assortment of shops and restaurants, each decorated in a bright Southwestern color scheme, almost like a row of peacocks, each trying harder than the last to attract the most tourist dollars. Xavier took note of all the different colors as he walked down the sidewalk heading for the cafe. What he didn't notice though was that he also walked past an ATM, it's security camera keeping a watchful eye.

***

* * *

Almost instantly, the picture registered a hit with the facial recognition software and a screen in a dark room thousands of miles away lit up with the image. The face at the keyboard lifted up with a broad smile. His net had finally caught the elusive prey, now all he had to do was alert Marcus and his gang so that they could sweep into town and snatch him up. If they had followed his instructions and stayed in the general area, then they should be able to reach the target within the hour. His hand brushed pistachio shells from the table as it fumbled for the phone. This was turning into a good morning indeed...

***

Meanwhile, Xavier sat in the back booth of the small cafe he had found on Main Street. It was too early for the tourist to really start pouring in, so he had been able to acquire a prime seat in the back corner, from which he could survey the restaurant. He had ordered eggs over easy with bacon, hash browns and whole wheat toast with a glass of orange juice. As he ate his breakfast he couldn't help but be amused at the headlines on WNC about a 'huge disturbance' at the Georgia World Journalism Conference. They interviewed several witnesses who talked about hearing gunshots and then almost being trampled in a huge stampede of people. "If they only knew the truth." he thought. But luckily they didn't, and at this point hopefully never would. Once he got the security clearance from Stephen, he would dispose of the virus, and with any luck that would help sort out the mess at the Citadel. Either way, he would return to the Monastery, and if he was still in hot water with the Citadel, he would simply fade from sight forever. He had to admit to himself as he sopped up the egg yolk that he was starting to fancy that option, even if the food the monks cooked left a lot to be desired.

After breakfast, Xavier strolled leisurely through the downtown area. His shower earlier and his breakfast had helped lift his spirits so he decided he would take a look around. He normally didn't have time to indulge in this type of activity, but since he was in a holding pattern there didn't seem to be any harm in checking out the local scenery. The morning sun was heating up though, and the tourist were starting to show up in droves, so after a short jaunt, Xavier decided it was better to cut his sight seeing short and retreat back to the warehouse. As he made his way past the shops, a woman suddenly burst out of a doorway carrying a plethora of bags under her arms. Xavier managed to dodge her, but bumped into the assortment of bags she was carrying, causing several of them to scatter on the sidewalk.

"I'm terribly sorry, how clumsy of me!" remarked Xavier, as he retrieved the bags from the ground and turned to hand them back to her.

The woman mumbled her thanks, while also huffing a little about Xavier paying attention to where he was going, but he barely heard any of it. When he had turned, he had caught something out of the corner of his eye that had put him on alert. He couldn't quite place it, but he could have swore he saw a flicker of quick movement across the street. He stood for a few moments after the woman had left, scanning the opposite side of the street, waiting to see anything out of the ordinary. When he saw nothing he turned and began walking down the street, only now, though he still gave the appearance of casually strolling along, Xavier had shifted into a different mindset entirely. As he drifted down the street, he began scanning every reflective surface to try to confirm what his instincts were telling him. A glance in a shop window confirmed what he feared, a young man in dark clothing was following him from the opposite side of the street. A few minutes later, the reflection Xavier caught in a car side mirror confirmed that he had not one, but two pursuers. The thought occurred to him that he could work his way back to his car, draw the pursuers away from the warehouse, and handle the problem outside of town. However, he didn't know exactly who or what he was dealing with at this point, so he decided that probably wasn't the best plan, plus he didn't want to take a chance and travel that far away from the virus, which was safely hidden back at the warehouse. One thing was for sure, he definitely needed to lure his followers back into the rundown section of town. He would have a far easier time dealing with them amongst the deserted buildings.

As Xavier approached the warehouse district, he couldn't help but notice the black SUV sitting on the side street. He remembered the moment on the highway where he had seen a black SUV in his rear view and the evasive maneuvers that he had taken to lose it. At the time he had worried that he was getting paranoid, but now he was sure he had been right all along. But how had they tracked him down? How were they here in Wingfield? He didn't have time to ponder these answers, he knew he was being stalked and they were just waiting for the best moment to ambush him. Rather than wait for them to make their move, Xavier decided he would take control of the situation and fight on his own terms.

Abruptly, he turned and quickly crossed a parking lot to an abandoned building. He popped the old, rusty lock in an instance and vanished into the dark interior. Motes of dust hung in the air and other than small shafts of filtered sunlight from the dirty windows high on the wall, it was draped in darkness and shadows. He couldn't have picked a more perfect setting. He settled back into the darkness and let his eyes adjust. Xavier had spent a great amount of time training to see in low light situations, so unless his pursuers had night vision goggles, he should have a distinct advantage. He also liked the layout of the building as it had long walkways divided by large shelves. No doubt they would split up and that's where his true advantage would lie.

Xavier stashed his duffle bag on a random shelf and lingered in the darkness, waiting on his would-be hunters to take the bait, when suddenly the front door burst open and a team of men spread out just inside. As he had hoped, they split off into groups and started fanning out to search the interior of the building. They continued to spread out as they began searching the warehouse, unaware that Xavier was slipping between the shelves and stacks of industrial equipment that were strewn about. One of the men moved too close to where Xavier was hiding and he sprang into action. In the near darkness he stepped out and with a quick strike, knocked the gun from the man's hand. Startled, the man spun and threw a wild back hand in an attempt to ward off Xavier's attack. Xavier easily ducked under the counter attack and wrapped his arms around the man's neck. With a quick wrenching motion, he heard vertebrae snap and immediately eased the now lifeless body to the floor. Without hesitation, Xavier left the body and moved through the shadows toward the approaching sound of footsteps.

Several aisles over he came upon another of his pursuers and quickly moved to ambush him. He grabbed the wrist of his victim's gun hand, pinning it back at an impossible angle. Just as Xavier reached back to grab a dagger from his jacket, he saw another mercenary appear from around the corner. Quickly, he pivoted his body and twisted the wrist of the man he held in his grip, while also exerting pressure on the elbow, so that the gun lined up with the advancing attacker. He squeezed the trigger, blowing a fine red mist from the back of the second man's head as the bullet passed through his skull. Just as quickly, Xavier pivoted back and switched the pressure from the outer elbow to the interior and caused the man's arm to point the gun back at his own head. Xavier squeezed the trigger once again and with a flash, blood and graymatter splattered against the shelves of the warehouse. Xavier let the body drop, knowing that the gunshots had taken away his element of surprise. He stepped to slip back into the darkness and regroup, when a third mercenary sprang from nowhere and swung the butt of his gun at Xavier's head. At the last second, Xavier pulled a cable from his sleeve, blocked the strike, and with one motion, knocked the gun from the attacker's hand. Quickly he slid past a second attempted strike by the assailant, wrapped the steel cable around the man's neck, and began to choke him out. He struggled against Xavier, but started to slump and lose strength as his consciousness slipped away. Just as he was almost out, the two combatants were caught in a pair of thin flashlight beams.

"Don't move! Let him go!" yelled a voice from behind Xavier.

Xavier glanced over his shoulder and saw the two men approaching. As they got close, he saw them nod and stiffen up, bracing to fire. At that moment, he took a deep breath, and spun just as they fired, their shots striking their own man. Xavier let the man drop to the floor as he stepped back into the shadows.

"What the hell? Nobody is that fast!" said one of the men, as he moved forward.

"Wait," yelled his partner, who had hung back slightly, but it was too late. Xavier had drawn his katana from it's special holster under his jacket, and while the first man moved forward sweeping his flashlight back and forth, he never saw Xavier step from behind a column to his right. One swing and his body slumped to the ground, his head falling beside it. Without hesitation, Xavier kicked the head so that it skidded across the floor toward the other would-be assailant. Just as he had hoped, the man saw the movement and swung his flashlight beam to see what it was. When the light fell on the head, he froze and Xavier closed the distance in an instance. Too late, he swung his flashlight beam up and saw Xavier looming just in front of him. Before he could squeeze the trigger, Xavier delivered a quick slash of the sword and both the gun and the hand holding it scattered across the floor. Xavier arched his sword up and brought it across in a powerful horizontal slash, taking the man's head off his body. It slumped to the floor, blood pouring from the stump, the head laying just off to the side, lit by the scattered spotlights from the two guns that were strewn in the aisle way.

The head stared back at him from the floor, eerily lit by the spotlight of the gun. Xavier stood and stared at the face for a few seconds before it dawned on him. He knew this man from the security footage that Vincent Guererro had provided moments before destroying himself and the laboratory back in Masaya. So this was the Brotherhood. Xavier had thought it was too easy to take them out. If they had been from the Citadel, it would have been much more difficult. But it also didn't make sense that the Brotherhood was able to track him down. Everything about them screamed small time operation, but yet they had been able to track him across the country, as well as find him again, even after he had lost them on the highway. It needed to be looked into further, and he was hoping that Stephen would have more info next time he contacted him, but for now he needed to get his bag and leave the warehouse. The area was relatively deserted, but the unanticipated gunfire could have still drawn some unwanted attention. Xavier moved around the room, turned off both flash lights. Afterwards he quickly wiped his katana with a rag from the shelf and put it away. Retrieving his duffle bag from the shelf he had hidden it on, he started for the door. He hated that he didn't have time to clean up this mess, and without the Citadel backing him, he couldn't order a cleanup crew. He was going to have to just leave the bodies and hope by the time anyone found them, he was far away. Stephen couldn't get that security clearance to him soon enough. Pausing at the front door, he considered going back to try to conceal the bodies. He also considered searching them for more info, to try to connect the dots, but ultimately he decided against it, his mission depended on destroying the virus as soon as he could. The longer it took, the more complicated things would get. Opening the front door to leave, the sunlight blinded him for a moment as his eyes struggled to adjust after being in the dark interior for so long. Just as he stepped out the door into the light he heard a voice bark out, "Freeze! Yavapai County Sheriff Department!"

CHAPTER TWELVE

Meet Bill Logan

Xavier's meditation was broken by the sound of a door opening and the loud clunk of boots walking across the hardwood floor. He opened his eyes and looked past the group of deputies, who were still staring at the oddity in the holding cell, and looked toward the man that had walked through the door. He was easily over six foot four inches tall, not counting the white stetson sitting on top of his head. He wore a dark blue suit, no tie and a large western belt buckle with not an ounce of irony. He glanced toward the holding cell, for a brief second holding Xavier in his gaze. His eyes were intense, but with just the slightest hint of humor, as if he was thinking of some joke that only he would get. He pulled a folder out from under his arm and waved it at Xavier before disappearing into an office with the Sheriff. The door went shut behind them and Xavier was left alone with the deputies again. He had always thought of himself as an extremely patient man, but even he had his limits. He thought back to the way the man had laughed so hard at his misfortune over the phone and felt annoyance growing inside him. He had to be careful, red flags had gone off when Agent Logan had suddenly decided to come down and handle the whole affair in person. But what could Xavier do? He had chosen this path. He could have dealt with the officers in a more direct, and decidedly deadly manner, but that wasn't who he was anymore. Unfortunately his current path seemed to move at a far slower pace than he had anticipated and he was feeling very exposed. As he knew from experience, in this business you could die of exposure.

Before he could get too lost in thought, the door to the office swung open and the Sheriff walked out, along with Agent Logan. The Sheriff immediately walked to the cell and unlocked the door. Xavier stepped out cautiously as the Sheriff extended his hand.

"Well I'm man enough to admit when I'm wrong, Agent Logan's vouched for you and he has the proper credentials, so you're free to go," said the Sheriff, as he unlocked the handcuffs and gave Xavier's hand a powerful shake.

"Although I will say that after seeing what I saw in that warehouse, I'm damn glad you're on our side," the Sheriff pulled Xavier a little closer, "And, I will expect you to finish your business and put this town in your rearview as quickly as possible, if you know what I mean."

Xavier was amused by the Sheriff's bravado and protectiveness for his people, "Sheriff I can assure you that is exactly what I plan to do. I'm just glad we could get everything straightened out."

Xavier released the Sheriff's hand and turned toward the tall cowboy to his right. He extended his hand, "Agent Bill Logan, pleased to meet you, sorry about earlier, I have a particularly dry sense of humor. No harm, right?"

"Now that I'm out of that cell, you have fully redeemed yourself in my eyes, Agent. I do appreciate your help in this matter," replied Xavier, while warily surveying the room. "Although I do question the reasoning behind you coming in person. It seems like an awful lot of trouble to go through when a phone call could have probably sufficed."

Agent Logan chuckled a little to himself, "Have you looked around much since you've been here Xavier? If you have you'll notice there's not a lot of anything. It's pretty quiet out here and it's easy for someone like me to get bored. When I got your call and looked over your file I was fascinated. Not by what was in it, mind you, but what wasn't in it. You see I get assigned all the time to act as liaison for various agencies, but I've never had a file so utterly empty. So given my light caseload as of late, I couldn't possibly turn down the opportunity to see a real life 'ghost' now could I?"

Xavier was about to reply when the Sheriff suddenly cleared his throat.

"I hate to interrupt but what are we supposed to do about the crime scene?"

"Oh, no worries," replied Agent Logan. "We have a team coming down to take care of that. It'll be like it never existed. Just leave it be and make sure no one else finds it before we clean it up."

With that the Sheriff signaled to one of his deputies and started back toward the office. Xavier started to call after him, "Excuse me, I still need to retrieve my things if you don't mind?"

Agent Logan cut him off, "No need, I've already taken the liberty of having your stuff loaded into the trunk of my car."

Xavier pondered the situation carefully as he followed Agent Logan out of the office. While this seemed incredibly odd, he was still basically in a holding pattern waiting on the package to arrive. The Agent may have an agenda, but Xavier decided it better to let it play out.

He followed Agent Logan out to his car, a standard issue sedan, and reluctantly climbed in the passenger's seat.

"So how about we grab a bite to eat?" asked Logan as he adjusted a pair of shades that looked like he stole them from a Texas State Trooper.

"Agent Logan, I appreciate your generosity for coming to get me out of that mess, but I must insist that I be allowed to continue on with my mission. The quicker I can move on and get away from this town, the better it will be for everyone," replied Xavier, trying to keep his voice even and ignore the growing annoyance he felt in the pit of his stomach.

"And I understand that," started Agent Logan, seemingly oblivious to Xavier's growing impatience, "But all I'm asking for is one sit down. That's it. You have to understand that I pride myself on being like an old bloodhound, in the sense that I can dig up info on anyone. I've had classified types before but I've always been able to get some feel for the person before I met up with them. With you though, it's just a blank file, not only that, but any attempt I made to find out any hint of info on you came back blank. You are for all intents and purposes a real life ghost and I have to admit, I'm completely fascinated. When the best researcher in the entire FBI can't find a single clue about your existence, that's something. So I came down here so I could see for myself." Logan gave Xavier a warm smile as he started the car.

Xavier was starting to feel a little too exposed. If this Agent had thrown his name around too much, the wrong people were going to notice. Cautiously he replied, "Agent that's all well and good, but I must ask you, did you keep this whole situation confidential? It is critical to my operation that no one, no matter who they work for, be informed of my whereabouts."

Logan nodded, "Yeah I did. I would never do anything to jeopardize your mission, whatever it may be. Everything has been strictly by the book." Xavier doubted anything this guy did was strictly by the book but decided against pressing the point.

The car rolled to a stop at an intersection and Xavier motioned toward the back of the car, "Agent I thank you for your generosity, but if you'll just let me out here, I'll collect my things and be on my way."

Agent Logan reached up and rubbed his chin for a second before letting the car move forward through the intersection. "Oh come on man, I've driven for hours just to get down here and meet you. At least satisfy my curiosity with one meal, that's all I ask. I haven't eaten today and I'm starving. What do you say? One meal, then you can get your stuff out of the trunk and be on your way." Logan glanced over at Xavier in the passenger's seat. It was impossible for Xavier to tell what was going on behind those mirrored shades but ultimately he decided to let it go. He still wasn't sure whether the Agent had an angle he was working or if he really was just curious and bored. In any case, he would let it play out and see where it took him.

"Okay fine," he finally replied, "One meal, what can it hurt?"

"Excellent!" replied Logan, "I know just the place out toward the edge of town, I passed it on the way in."

Xavier looked out the window at the brightly painted tourist shops, all decorated up to entice the tourist into the trap. At the time, Xavier wondered if he and the tourist had something in common...

CHAPTER THIRTEEN

Last Meal?

Carol's Diner sat on the outskirts of town, not too far from the warehouse district, but slightly remote. It had the look of your typical American diner with gleaming, shiny metal walls and big front windows. As Logan and Xavier walked inside they were greeted by music from the early era of rock and roll and decor that was a nod to the nearby Route 66. It's narrow room was lined on one side by booths with a classic counter on the opposite side with a few tables on the far end of the room. Xavier noticed as they entered that the place seemed empty except for the waitress and an elderly lady sitting in a booth near the door.

Agent Logan walked through to the far wall and sat down with his back to the wall, a move which forced Xavier to sit with his back to the room. A red flag went off in Xavier's well trained mind. He didn't like sitting with his back to the room because it left him vulnerable and Agent Logan, having also been a trained agent, would have to know this as well. He wondered if he was overanalyzing the situation as he sat down and took the menu that Logan offered him. The waitress came and took their drink orders, with Logan having a Coke and Xavier a water. They sat in silence staring down at their menus and the awkward silence stretched on. It was while pretending to peruse the menu, that Xavier noticed a slight bulge under Agent Logan's left underarm and when Logan fidgeted about, getting more comfortable on the bench seat, he caught the most fleeting of glimpses at a large handgun, possibly a .357. He made no mention of it and continued to feign interest in the menu. The waitress returned with their drinks and asked for their orders. Logan glanced at Xavier, who didn't look up and proceeded with his order.

"I'll have the pork chop with mashed potatoes and green beans, please ma'am," said Logan with a quick wink to the waitress.

"Sure thing, dear and what about you sir?" asked the waitress.

Xavier glanced once more over the menu, "I'll have the steak, rare with steamed carrots, green beans, and a side salad."

"You got it, we'll have it right up for you," replied the waitress.

As she turned to leave Xavier interjected, "Oh miss, pardon me, but could I change the salad and get the tomato soup instead?"

The waitress nodded and scribbled down the change as she was walking away. Logan sat for a second looking off into the distance and finally spoke. "Hey look, I would like to apologize for the way I laughed at you on the phone, I really didn't mean any harm by it, but you have to admit it was a very odd situation."

Xavier looked at the Agent's smiling eyes and strangely enough felt himself warming slightly to this odd, western throwback. His mind still raced, weighing evidence, was it a trap? Or was this a case of his paranoia getting the better of him? He smiled the slightest of smiles and nodded.

"It's alright Agent Logan," came the reply. "I have to admit, it was a very peculiar situation I found myself in. It was a rare moment of carelessness on my part and I apologize for it taking up so much of your time, as well as taking you so far away from your office."

Xavier continued to feign a smile and his words seemed to relax the agent, as he sat back a little while chewing his lip, before leaning in again. "So look," Logan began. "Just what kind of situation did you get yourself into in that warehouse? If the sheriff's account is to be believed, it looked like a regular slaughterhouse."

The smile dropped and Xavier's eyes went cold as they once again bore into Logan. "Agent Logan, as you probably can guess, I'm not at liberty to say much, if anything. The warehouse was an unfortunate mishap and I required your help to get out of jail, for which I'm grateful, but beyond that I cannot elaborate any further."

Agent Logan again rubbed his chin and thought on it, "Well can I assume it was some sort of ambush? Who ambushed you? I mean you realize that we're gonna have a team clean it up so I'm gonna find all of this out eventually."

Xavier again gave the slightest of smiles, "And by that time, I'll be long gone." The agent smiled again, only this time Xavier thought it was starting to resemble the smile of a crocodile before it sprung on its prey.

"So, what exactly is it that you do?" asked Agent Logan.

Xavier stared at Logan for several moments before totally ignoring the question. "How long have you worked as an FBI agent?"

Logan shifted in his chair again, and again there was the slightest glimpse of the handgun under his arm. "Well, it's been 10 years ago last month. I started off in the Dallas, Texas office and bounced around a little here and there, before ending up in Phoenix."

Xavier smiled, "Yes that explains it. I've been trying to figure it out. You don't seem much like the typical FBI agent, but the Dallas connection ties everything together nicely." Logan grinned and Xavier considered his next words carefully and decided to prod a little.

"Yes it all makes sense now, the boots, the belt buckle, the cowboy hat... and the six shooter." At the mention of the gun a look briefly went over Logan's face, like clouds over a troubled sea, Xavier had definitely caught him off guard.

Then the smile slowly spread back across his face and the lines calmed. "Well, you certainly have an eye for detail Xavier." He then almost subconsciously adjusted his jacket, pulling it slightly closer as if to better conceal the weapon.

Xavier appeared calm to the world, but inside he was on high alert. From that exchange he had seen enough subtle signals to know that this wasn't a simple lunch. He was starting to suspect that Agent Logan was merely stalling. As he was running over options in his head, the waitress suddenly appeared with their food.

"Will you be needing any steak sauce?" asked the waitress.

"No ma'am, this will do nicely, thank you," replied Xavier as he reached and picked up the napkin holder to retrieve a napkin from it. As he sat it down he nonchalantly turned the holder so that the polished silver side faced him, giving him a somewhat distorted view of the room behind him. A glance confirmed that the old woman was still sitting in the booth near the door. The two sat in silence again as they dug into their food. Finally Logan spoke up again, "So what would you have done if you couldn't reach me from the Sheriff's office?"

Xavier glanced up from his steak, "It would have depended on how the situation played itself out. As I mentioned, I'm on a tight schedule and the longer I stay exposed, the more likely I would have attracted the wrong type of attention."

Logan prodded further, "Sounds like you must have some real

heavy hitters looking for you and your cargo."

Xavier abruptly put down his fork and stared intensely at Agent Logan, "I never mentioned any cargo, agent."

The two men stared at each other and Logan finally spoke, "Look, I get the impression that you're a pretty good guy, despite the line of work you're in. You could have probably dusted the sheriff and his troupe of boy scouts but you didn't, that says a lot to me. Instead you wasted most of your day waiting for me to come get you out of jail in order to protect them. I can appreciate that, but I'm afraid I can't let you leave here today with the cargo you're carrying." Xavier glanced in the napkin holder and noticed the old lady had gotten up from her booth and was slowly making her way toward them.

Logan continued, "Like I said, I appreciate your character, so I'm gonna offer you a deal. I have a team that's going to be here any minute to interrogate you about the whereabouts of 'Tears of the Dragon', but it doesn't have to go down like that. If you give it to me now, I'll let you walk and I'll just tell them you got the jump on us. We get what we want, and you get to disappear back into the shadows. What do you say?" Agent Logan glanced past Xavier and he noticed in the reflection that the lady had stopped about halfway across the room from them.

Xavier sat staring at the agent for several long moments before he finally spoke, "Agent, I appreciate the kind words. I know that this is just business and I appreciate your offer, as well as your honesty. And since you've been honest with me, I'll be totally honest with you as well." Xavier paused, checking the reflection and looked back at Agent Logan, "I hate tomato soup."

Suddenly Xavier flung the bowl of hot soup in Logan's face and kicked the table up against the agent, pinning his arms to his side. The old lady approached from behind and tried to grab Xavier but in an instant, he shifted out of his seat while simultaneously twisting her arm, throwing her headfirst into Agent Logan. Their heads cracked and she fell onto the table causing it to tilt further down onto his arms.

"Get the hell off of me!" He screamed as she rolled backwards off the table, allowing her wig to fall to the floor revealing her jet black hair and pulling her gun from beneath her skirt. Agent Logan erupted upward, sending the table and all of it's contents scattering across the floor of the restaurant. He grabbed his gun and together they swept the room. It was silent except for the jukebox that continued to play the golden oldies. Xavier had vanished and the room was empty except for the waitress, who slowly peeked her head up from behind the counter, before getting one look at the agents with their guns drawn and dropping back out of view.

***

Moments later they stood outside of the restaurant staring at Logan's car. The window was smashed out, the trunk was open, Xavier's bag and belongings were gone and several of the tires were slashed. Logan stood with a look of disbelief on his face.

"What the hell? Nobody is that fast... How the hell did he get out the door and do all this before we could catch up with him?"

Logan looked the car over for a second before the frustration of the situation caught up with him.   Suddenly he kicked the tire and pounded on the roof of the car.

"Shit! Shit! Shit! Shit!"

"Get a hold of yourself Bill!" yelled the now dark haired, decidedly not old, female agent. Agent Stacy Martinez was Bill Logan's partner and used to his unorthodox ways, as well as his occasional temper tantrums.

"How the hell did all this go down anyway? We were just supposed to keep him under surveillance until the rest of the team arrived. Was it so hard just to have lunch and make small talk?"

Logan paced for a few moments before tipping back his hat and scratching his head. "He never bought it," he replied, as much to himself as to her. "He was suspicious from the start, besides making small talk with a mannequin would be easier than trying to get anything out of him. I let him get under my skin and got impatient, but I figured with the two of us in close quarters we could handle it."

"Wild Bill strikes again..." quipped Agent Martinez.

"Don't start that shit, you were supposed to stay at the door." snapped Agent Logan, as he pulled out his phone. He dialed a number and waited impatiently while it rang a few times.

"George Wilkins," came the reply from the other end of the call.

"George, how far out are you?" asked Logan.

"About ten minutes or so, what's up?"

"He got the jump on us, totally unexpected," explained Logan while deflecting a look from Agent Martinez. "Get here as quick as you can, we can't let him get too much of a head start."

He snapped the phone shut and looked at Agent Martinez. "Fan out and search the area, look for any signs of him. And for god sakes, if you find him, call for backup, do not try to take him alone, understand?"

Martinez nodded and sprinted around the back of the restaurant toward the alley way. Agent Logan stood staring at what was left of his car. He had underestimated Xavier Greene, he didn't intend on making the same mistake twice.

CHAPTER FOURTEEN

Tracking a Ghost

Six minutes later, George Wilkins and the rest of the strike team pulled up in front of the diner in a large black sprinter van. Clouds of dust swirled off the parking lot, but Agent Logan barely noticed. He had to admit he felt better about the situation now that the rest of the team was there. He had badly underestimated Xavier Greene, and he and Martinez had let him slip away. Although he didn't know what Xavier was, he knew that he was good, possibly way better than he had let on. Not only had he gotten away from two armed agents in a small room, he had retrieved his things from the trunk of the car and disabled it in an impossibly short amount of time. He had thought he was stringing Xavier along, but the whole time he had been biding his time, waiting to see Logan's hand. Once Logan divulged their true mission, he merely left. That was the hardest part to get over. He was a ten year veteran of the FBI and Martinez was no slouch either and yet Xavier handled them like a couple of kids before disappearing without a trace.

"Hey boss, what's the deal?" said George Wilkins, as he jumped down out of the truck.

Logan looked up from the map he had spread out on the trunk of his car. "He got the jump on us and flat out vanished. Martinez and I swept the immediate area and found no sign of him. Fortunately, Martinez slipped a tracker in his bag, while I was stalling at the Sheriff's office. Now that you guys are here we should be able to track him."

"Way to go Martinez, sharp thinking!" said George, winking at Martinez.

Martinez laughed, "Someone's got to keep him straight." She quickly retrieved a laptop from the back of the sprinter and started booting it up.

George glanced at Logan's car, "Jeez, looks like you parked on the wrong side of town homie." He winced as he looked at the huge gashes in the tires, "Holy shit, how did he slash the tires like that?"

Logan shook his head, "This guy's a piece of work. Looks like a funeral director. The most unusual part is he wasn't carrying a gun. Only a variety of hand to hand weapons and a, get this, short katana that apparently he wears under his jacket."

"Bringing a knife to a gun fight ain't good policy," quipped George, still staring at the eviscerated tires.

"Maybe," responded Logan, "but apparently he took out a whole gang of well armed thugs at a warehouse in town, so I wouldn't take it too lightly."

George shook his head and walked off to get a report from the rest of the team, who had fanned out to survey the scene and the inside of the diner for fingerprints and DNA.

A few minutes later he returned. "Got some partial prints from your car and the silverware, but we'll have to sort out what's yours and what's his since everything got flung all over the place. What did you guys do, try to apprehend him with your superior food fighting skills?"

"Very funny," replied Logan, as he rubbed his neck, trying to stave off a stress induced headache. "Like I said he got the jump on us, which is why my shirt and jacket are covered in tomato soup. Just run the prints and let me know what you find."

Just then Martinez finally looked up from the laptop, "Um, so didn't you refer to this guy as a ghost?"

"Yeah," said Logan, suddenly apprehensive because of the puzzled look Martinez was giving him.

"Well, I'm beginning to believe he actually is one," said Martinez as she slowly turned the laptop around.

On the screen was a map of the town but no marker to signify Xavier's current location. The map was blank.

"It's like he vanished into thin air," said Martinez as Logan just stared at the screen.

"Son of a- how can that happen? Did you check the tracer before you slipped it into his stuff?" asked Logan as he felt the growing headache starting to creep into his temples.

"I checked everything. I've even rebooted the program three times. There is absolutely no trace of him," said Martinez. "I mean, it's possible that he found the tracer and got rid of it, but even if he did, I doubt he would take the time to destroy it. He was already in a huge hurry to get away."

The three of them stood staring at the computer for a few moments before George spoke up. "So what's the plan now boss?"

Logan shrugged his shoulders. "There aren't many options. It's not like we can go door to door looking for him. Best guess is that we should head toward that warehouse and try to find some clues there."

Just then, the computer beeped and Martinez quickly spun it around.

"Looks like our luck is improving! I just got a signal from the tracer and it appears to be near the warehouse where he had his altercation this morning!"

"George, take the team in the sprinter, Martinez and I will take her car and meet you near the warehouse," said Logan as he grabbed a bag from the trunk of his car and slung it over his shoulder.

About ten minutes later, Logan and Martinez met George and the rest of the team around the corner from the warehouse. George had already scouted the area when Logan approached the rear of the sprinter where the team was gearing up.

"Okay, we've got exits on the front and back of the building, as well as a loading dock," said George as Logan looked over photos of the building on George's phone.

"Is he still in there?" Logan asked Martinez as she brought the tracking program online.

"Affirmative. From the looks of it, he's upstairs in a central office," replied Martinez.

Logan nodded as the outlines of a plan started to form in his head.

"Okay, here is the drill. Martinez, you and George take the team and come in the ground level. Cover all the exits and work your way up. Use extreme caution as I don't need to remind you, he has already taken out six heavily armed people today and overpowered two Federal agents. I put a call in to the office on the way here and requested additional backup and a containment crew in the event anything goes wrong with the cargo he is carrying. I'm going to head in from the top, with the intention of driving him down into your waiting arms. Any questions?"

"Yeah just one," replied Martinez. "When did you learn to fly?"

George chuckled, "She's got a point, boss. There are no fire escapes on that building or did you miss that?"

Logan grinned. "No, you are correct, there are no fire escapes on that building. However, there are fire escapes on the building beside of it. And the alley way is pretty narrow, it should be a piece of cake."

Martinez rolled her eyes as Logan retrieved a lasso from the bag in the back seat. "Here we go again," she quipped.

"Hey, you have to admit, it'll give me the element of surprise. I'm tired of this guy outmaneuvering us at every turn, and I don't want to add another single person to his daily totals." Logan put a pair of gloves in his pocket, threw the lasso over his shoulder and headed toward the building.

Martinez and the rest of the team watched as Logan worked his way up to the top of the rusted, old fire escape. Once at the top, he had to admit this plan didn't seem as good as it had from the ground. The other building was one story higher and the alley way looked a lot wider than when he had viewed it from below. But, he pulled out the lasso, double checked the knot, and slipped on his gloves, as he tried to push thoughts of a four story fall to the asphalt out of his head. When everything checked out okay he scanned the top of the building across the alleyway and spotted a vent pipe sticking out the top of the building. He began spinning the lasso, slowly at first, then faster as he began to build up momentum. Finally he flung the lasso across the alley and nailed the pipe. He gave the rope a sharp tug to tighten it and, with one last glance at the team watching him from below, Logan stepped up onto the railing and flung himself off into space. He swung out over the alley way and put his boots up to block as much impact as he could. He crunched up against the brick wall and almost lost his grip on the rope, but managed to stabilize himself when he found his footing on a row of decorative bricks that seemed to have been put in to signify the difference between floors in the building. He hung there for a few seconds getting his bearings, then put his feet firmly against the building and started walking while pulling himself up with the rope. His knees were on fire within the first few steps, and his elbows felt like they would explode. It had been a while since he had climbed a rope, and he thought about the fact that this would have been much easier ten years ago. Finally, he pulled himself up over the roof of the building and collapsed in a heap. After a few seconds he raised up and looked over the side, down at his team and gave them the thumbs up.

"Son of a bitch, he really did it," said George as he returned the gesture.

"Yep, 'Wild Bill' strikes again. Now let's move out," said Martinez, as she checked her weapon. The team assembled outside of the front door, George quickly picked the lock and the team rushed in, never noticing the tiny sensor, hidden in the dust beside the door.

CHAPTER FIFTEEN

With Backup like this...

Xavier Greene darted back and forth in the dim light of the office he had called home for the last few days. He rolled up his bed roll and stuffed it into a large duffle bag, while scanning through the other things he had laid out. After his encounter with the FBI, Xavier had decided that a change in location would be in order. He had taken a chance calling the FBI to start with, but he hadn't anticipated them knowing about his deadly cargo. How could they have possibly known? The only thing he could come up with was that someone was pulling the strings and the FBI were just a pawn to help them flush him out. In any case, Xavier knew that the agents would waste little time in trying to find him, and the warehouse district would be a logical place to start. Even if they did go to the scene of his incident from this morning, he had an insurmountable head start. While they were looking for clues, he was almost packed, and they had no idea where he was. He packed a few more tools into his bag, when suddenly the alarm for the motion sensors he installed downstairs buzzed repeatedly in his pocket. Xavier pulled out the remote and checked the lights. There were breaches at the front doors. How could they have gotten here so fast? His gaze fell on the bag that he had been carrying with him when he was picked up by the sheriff. Quickly Xavier grabbed the bag and checked the contents. At the bottom, under his change of clothes, was a small, inconspicuous device with a blinking blue light. Xavier sighed and dropped the tracker to the floor, crushing it with his heel. The stress of this mission was getting to him, and this was the second critical error he had made today. Perhaps if he made it through this, retirement to the monastery wouldn't be such a bad idea. Xavier shook his head at the thought and hastily threw the rest of his stuff into his duffle bag. It really didn't matter at this point, they had found him but as usual, he had an exit strategy, and would be long gone before they knew what happened. With everything packed he took one last look around the room, walked over to a large filing cabinet and opened the middle drawer to reveal a padded box. Just as he lifted the box he heard the sound of a revolver cocking and froze.

"Don't move," growled Logan as he leveled his .357 at Xavier's head.

"Is this about the soup?" quipped Xavier as he slowly raised his hands.

"No, it's about keeping the country safe, now put your hands behind your back, slowly," came the reply.

Xavier complied and lowered his hands behind his back. "Then I would think we have the same mission, although if you think the people calling your shots care about the safety of the people of this country or any other then you're either deliriously naive or delusional."

Logan fastened the handcuffs on Xavier's wrists and with a quick foot to the back of his leg, he dropped Xavier abruptly to his knees.

"It's definitely about the soup…" mused Xavier. After a pause he continued, "Logan if you are really concerned about the safety of the country you wouldn't interfere in my mission. I must be allowed to carry it out."

"Don't start that shit, I underestimated you the first time, I don't plan on doing it again," said Logan as he looked around the room. "In fact, I even took the precaution on the way over here to call for backup. They're sending a hazmat squad out as we speak to make sure nothing happens with that cargo of yours."

A grave look of concern crossed Xavier's face as Logan continued to look about the room.

"Wait, you called for backup? Over a cell phone?" A sense of urgency grew in Xavier's voice. "Agent Logan, you must release me, we're all in great danger. If your conversation was monitored then I'm afraid backup isn't the only thing that is on it's way. We have to move quickly." As he spoke Xavier started to rise to his feet but stopped abruptly when Logan leveled his gun to his head. He slowly lowered back down to his knees.

"I told you, no more tricks Xavier. We played footsie all day and all that got me was a ruined suit and a vandalized vehicle."

Xavier stared at Logan intensely with steely eyes. "Agent, there are far more powerful people who want to take the cargo before I can destroy it. If they find us here, they will kill us all, including your team."

Logan shook his head, "So you're telling me that there is some organization capable of tapping the FBI's phones and intercepting a team of elite FBI agents? Even for you, that's far-fetched."

Slowly the sound of a helicopter began to fade in before building to a rhythmic throbbing that shook the room.

Xavier raised his eyebrows, "Isn't this a little soon for your backup?"

Logan considered the situation as he chewed his lip. "Yeah, actually it is, and they shouldn't be arriving by helicopter."

The sounds of boots resonated down the hall outside the room. Suddenly, the door burst open and the room was flooded by a team of soldiers in black with machine guns drawn. Logan pointed his gun at the men and was answered by a chorus of laser sights focusing on his chest and head. Slowly he uncocked and lowered his weapon. "Easy fellas, we're all on the same side. " Logan explained.

The men continued holding Logan in their sights, when a tall man with silver hair and a salt and pepper beard entered the room. With a motion of his hand he called the men off.

"Agent Logan? I'm Bill Mikelson, sergeant first class, special forces." He extended his hand and Logan shook it.

"Sorry for the hostile reaction Sergeant, I wasn't expecting a special forces squad, I thought we ordered a hazmat team?" as he looked the man over. He seemed special forces or at least some kind of hardened soldier. His face was rugged and hard with a diagonal scar on the left side of his forehead.

"Yes sir you did," the man responded with a grin. "As it happens my squad has special training in hazardous materials and we were the closest available unit. We had actually been training in the desert not far from here when we got the call. We're supposed to secure the virus until the actual hazmat unit gets here."

This explanation seemed to ease Logan slightly. "Well I'm glad you're here Sergeant and will appreciate your assistance."

Bill Mikelson motioned towards Xavier, "Okay a couple of you men find a chair and let's get the prisoner set up for interrogation so we can ascertain the location of the biological element."

Logan interrupted, "Um, Sergeant that may not be necessary, when I entered the room I caught the suspect opening that drawer in the file cabinet and as you can see there is a padded box, which I'm assuming may be our cargo."

Bill walked over to the drawer and picked up the box, turning it over in his hand and examining the large biohazard label affixed to the outside.

"Good work, Agent. Excellent work, in fact." While looking at the box, Bill made a nonchalant hand gesture and suddenly a soldier drove the butt of his rifle into the back of Logan's head. Logan collapsed to the ground in a heap as the soldiers took his gun and fastened his hands behind his back with a zip tie.

Bill Mikelson glanced over his shoulder at Logan before turning his gaze back to the package in his hands. He reached up and touched his ear piece.

"The package is secure, tie up the loose ends."

Immediately the rapid pop of gunshots could be heard coming from below them on the lower floors of the building. Logan laid on the floor, his head feeling like it was gonna explode. Through his hazy vision he could see Xavier, still on his knees facing him. Xavier was moving his lips, but Logan couldn't quite make it out. He struggled to bring himself back further into consciousness. He could hear the gunshots, and he thought of Martinez and George, who were probably fighting for their lives at this moment. The thoughts of his teammates brought him back through the fog and he once again looked at Xavier. He was finally able to make out two words that Xavier seemed to be repeating to him,

"Stay down!"

Bill Mikelson sat the padded box down on a table and flipped the latch. When he opened the top a pressurized stream of liquid shot out of the container and struck him in the face. He screamed as smoke encompassed his head and his skin bubbled. Simultaneously, Xavier rolled backwards and rolled his hands down the back of his leg and over his feet so that they were no longer behind his back. He then leapt to his feet and struck the nearest soldier in the throat with his still handcuffed hands. Wrapping his arms around the soldier's arm and gun, he squeezed the trigger on the rifle and swept it around the room, taking out the startled squad of soldiers. Xavier then flipped the soldier's arm back so the machine gun hooked under the soldier's chin and fired one last burst, dropping the soldier's now slumping body to the ground.

Xavier stood for a few seconds surveying the room, littered with dead soldiers and the smoldering body of Bill Mikelson in the center of it all. He then glanced at Logan, who was still on the floor with his hands zip tied behind his back. Xavier raised his eyebrows at Logan and shrugged his shoulders, "With backup like this, who needs enemies?"

He then walked over to Logan and knelt in front of him, patting him down until he found the keys to the cuffs. "Still think you have the situation under control?" asked Xavier as he removed the cuffs from his wrists. He then turned Logan over and used a small dagger he pulled from his coat to cut the zip-tie from Logan's wrist.

Logan rolled over and rubbed his wrists, "Who are these guys?"

Xavier went back to quickly throwing the last few things in his bag, "I have no idea, although I suspect they intercepted your call back to the office and used that to get the jump on us."

Logan rose to his feet and looked around for his gun while Xavier was gathering his things. "I would thank you for saving my life, but from the looks of it, you had something different in mind for me." He nodded toward the smoldering remains of Bill Mikelson.

"Don't be ridiculous, Agent Logan. I would have warned you of the true contents of the box. You don't seem that bad, even if you are being used as a pawn in a much larger game. That man was a killer and got exactly what he deserved."

As he spoke Xavier walked over to a seemingly random spot on the floor. He knelt, pulled out the dagger again, and pried a small square out of the floorboard. Xavier reached into the hollow spot and retrieved a small padded box. Xavier examined the box briefly, before opening it and pulling out a small vial.

"This is what all the trouble is about Agent Logan. This is Tears of the Dragon, it was created in a lab in South America. If I were to open this vial right now, it would spread until it had wiped out most of the population of the world. My mission is to safeguard it until I reach the facility where it will be safely destroyed. Now do you see why my mission is so important? The Brotherhood would use it against mankind, the people that are fighting your team on the lower floors would use it as blackmail against the world. I cannot let this virus exist, it has to be destroyed." Xavier lowered the vial back into the padded box and after locking it, placed it in his jacket pocket. Just as he turned away to grab his bag, he heard the now familiar click of the hammer on Logan's gun.

"You know I can't let you do that Xavier. You may have your mission, and I think it's a noble one, but I have my orders, and that is to retrieve the virus and bring it back to my superiors." He leveled the gun at the back of Xavier's head as he spoke. "Now hand it over, this doesn't have to be messy. Give it to me and I'll let you walk, right now."

Xavier looked over his shoulder at Logan, his .357 aimed directly at him. He shook his head slowly. "Don't you have more pressing matters, such as the well being of your team?"

Logan turned his head and listened to the unrelenting gunfire echoing from the lower levels, he knew his team was in hot water, the thought of George or Martinez being in danger or worse, made his heart race. He turned back to Xavier to find the room empty, Xavier had vanished again. How could he have been so stupid as to turn his back on this guy? He swore under his breath and tapped his earpiece. Static was the only reply. He pulled the earpiece out, guessing that it was being scrambled, and ran for the stairs. He would catch up to Xavier later, right now he had to help the others, if it wasn't too late.

CHAPTER SIXTEEN

Enter the Silver Wraith

Downstairs, Stacy Martinez, George Wilkins, and Agent Matt Rollins ran through a gauntlet of gunfire, splintering wood, and shattering glass. Moments ago the soldiers, who had shown up suddenly and announced they were there to help secure the facility, had opened fire and it was a slaughter from the onset. The positions they had taken to 'secure the perimeter' had put them in the perfect position to catch the agents in a crossfire and most of them had gone down immediately. Martinez would've been among them if she hadn't noticed a soldier thumbing the safety off on his gun seconds before it went down. She had given a high sign to George just a split second before the shooting started, and they had somehow managed to avoid most of the fire. Now they were in a nonstop fight for their lives.

Turning a corner she blasted a soldier with a burst from her M4 as they dove through a doorway into an office. Scrambling across the floor of the office, The took shelter behind a desk and listened. The gunfire had stopped, but you could still hear the soldiers going room to room. Sooner or later they were going to find them.

Martinez checked her ammo. "Shit, one more burst and my automatic is done."

George Wilkins shook his head, "Yeah same here, soon we'll be down to sidearms only and that ain't gonna end well. Who the hell are these guys? Xavier's backup?"

Martinez wiped the sweat from her brow, "No, this doesn't seem his style. Besides, I got the distinct impression that he was working alone from the short time we got to observe him earlier."

"Well whoever they are, they're definitely not on our side," said

Matt Rollins. "We seriously need to get our ass out of here."

Martinez was about to reply when the office exploded around them. The automatic weapon fire shredded the flimsy glass windows and cheap wood veneer of the office.

"Quick this way!" shouted Martinez as she dove for a side door. Just as they made it through the doorway, several of the soldiers came crashing through what was left of the window pane onto the spot where the agents had been moments earlier. George and Stacy opened fire through the doorway and caught the soldiers off guard, dropping them where they stood. Both machine guns were empty and they tossed them aside, just as another soldier kicked the door open at the end of the hallway. He had them and they knew it. He raised his weapon to fire, when suddenly a single gunshot went off and the soldier fell to the floor. Behind him stood Bill Logan, his .357 smoking in his hand.

"How bad is it?" asked Logan.

"I think we're all that's left," said Martinez, "Where's Xavier?"

Logan shook his head, "He gave me the slip, we got ambushed by a squad of these goons. I thought we were done, but somehow Xavier turned it around and took them out."

"He took out a whole squad?" asked George, "What the hell is this guy?"

"We can figure that out later," replied Logan, "Right now we need to get the hell out of here and call in reinforcements. There appears to be a machine shop and loading dock back this way, if we can make it out the back entrance maybe we can lose them in the alleyways."

"Okay, Logan and I will take the lead," said Martinez, checking her sidearm, "George, you and Rollins take the rear, let's go."

The group quickly sprinted down a dark hallway, through a door, and down another short hallway that led to the machine shop. Just as Rollins and Wilkins neared the door, a shadow moved behind them. Rollins saw a flutter of silver mesh out of the corner of his eye and spun to fire, only to be caught by a curved sword stabbing through his midsection. George Wilkins turned in time to see the second blade slash through Rollins' neck. Blood gushed from the wound as he sunk to the floor, the arterial flow splattered on the front of the figure. In the dim light George couldn't make out it's face until it started walking toward him. It was tall, almost 7 feet, dressed head to toe in some kind of silver mesh, complete with a hood. It's face covered by a mirrored faceplate that dripped with the blood of Agent Rollins.

Across the machine shop, near the exit door, Xavier crouched in the shadows awaiting his chance to escape. He had been surprised to see that Agent Logan had made it to his friends and were already crossing the machine shop toward his position. He wasn't worried, as he had his exit strategy. After they escaped, he would slip off through a window he had left unlocked on the side of the building. He watched as Logan and a female agent, whom he recognized from the diner, crossed the machine shop. A third agent backed out the doorway firing his revolver when suddenly a curved blade sliced his gun hand off. A tall figure in silver stepped out the doorway and caught the agent by his neck between it's twin curved blades. Xavier's blood ran cold.

"It can't be," he thought as he watched the grisly scene in disbelief. He had heard many tales about this assassin, but had always assumed it was more myth than fact. And yet here it stood, the Silver Wraith, a name spoken in hushed voices around the underworld. Rumored to be indestructible, and as ruthless as it was unrelenting, Xavier had to admit the hair on the back of his neck was standing up. If what he had heard about the Wraith was true, they may all be lucky to make it out alive.

The Silver Wraith held George Wilkins between it's crossed blades, as if observing him, before simultaneously bringing the blades through his neck, completely severing his head from his body. George's body went limp and fell to the floor, blood gushing out onto the cold concrete.

Stacy screamed, "GEORGE! NOOOO!" and advanced on the Wraith, opening fire with her side arm. Three shots hit the Wraith dead center and it took half a step backwards, before advancing on Martinez. Undaunted she unloaded the rest of her sidearm into the Wraith, with her final shot hitting it in the faceplate. The shot to the faceplate sparked when it hit and knocked the Wraith's head back from the impact but it immediately righted itself and continued advancing on Martinez. She seemed to be in a daze, transfixed with a look of terror and disbelief on her face as she stood squeezing the trigger of the now empty gun. Logan suddenly appeared at her side and raised his .357, when suddenly Xavier jumped between the duo and the advancing Wraith.

Xavier put up a hand toward Logan, "Get to the door, quickly!" Logan bailed for the door as Xavier pulled his katana from under the back of his jacket. At the sight of the katana, the Wraith stopped advancing and cocked it's head to the side, as if puzzled by this new development. It spun it's twin blades once and dropped into an attack stance. It started to slowly circle towards Xavier. As he settled into a defensive stance, the Wraith altered it's stance to a different offensive position in order to better take advantage of Xavier's defense. The minute the Wraith changed it's stance however, Xavier also changed his to mirror a better defense. They continued circling in this dance of death, each making adjustments to mirror the other. Subtly, Xavier also slowly worked his way backwards until he was almost at the edge of the machine shop, near the open door through which Logan and Martinez had fled. He could hear the footsteps of the other soldiers coming down the hallways and knew he only had moments before they were overrun. Finally he and the Wraith stopped circling each other and stood rooted in place. The sweat dripped off Xavier as he stared at the Wraith, unmoving and unreadable, the blood of the agents it had just killed caking on the silver mesh of it's outfit. The Wraith moved, ever so slightly, and Xavier thought he could sense it tensing, like a coiled snake preparing to strike.

Suddenly a group of soldiers came barreling down the hallway behind the Wraith. At the appearance of the soldiers, the Wraith turned its head and held up a hand, with the curved sword still in it. The soldiers immediately fell back. It was clear that this was the Wraith's fight and they were to stay out of it. Xavier took advantage of the Wraith's momentary distraction and spun backwards, while simultaneously slashing the chain holding the counterweight for the fire doors that hung between the machine shop and the loading dock. The chain sparked and split from the specially hardened steel of the blade, releasing the heavy fire doors. Xavier rolled backwards under the dropping door, making through just as the door fell, cutting the Wraith off from them. He heard an impact where the Wraith hit the door from the inside, followed by gunshots echoing off the steel fire door. As he exited the open door, Xavier was surprised to see Logan and Martinez waiting nearby.

"I thought I told you to leave?" he yelled over the chaos of the gunfire ricocheting off the steel door.

"Yeah well, I didn't like your chances," replied Logan, "What the hell was that thing?"

"Trouble, big trouble, now follow me and let's get out of here!" replied Xavier as he shot past Logan and Martinez.

"That's the best idea I've heard all day," said Martinez as they followed Xavier down the alleyway.

Ryan McGinnis

CHAPTER SEVENTEEN

On the Run Again

The trio sprinted down the alleyway and ducked down another smaller alley where Xavier grabbed a large pry bar he had left behind a pile of old pallets. He then began working feverishly to remove a manhole cover in the center of the alley. After some effort, the cover came up and he slid it to the side and gestured for the others to enter. Logan and Martinez took the cue and climbed down into the sewer. As Xavier followed, he pulled the manhole shut behind them. They stood in the pitch black waiting for several seconds as the heavy pounding of boots on the pavement could be heard above them. After the steps had faded, Xavier tossed the crowbar to the side and turned on two flash lights, passing one to Logan. Xavier motioned for them to follow him and they started down the dark, dank, sewer tunnel.

After they had been walking for several minutes, Martinez remarked, "So this is why the tracking device didn't work. The sewer must've blocked the signal."

Xavier nodded but didn't reply, as they continued down the tunnel.

After a minute or so longer, Logan finally spoke up, "So I have a question, what the hell was up with the big silver weirdo from the warehouse? It took a whole clip from Martinez' gun and didn't even slow down. What the hell are we up against?"

Xavier glanced back over his shoulder, "Well, if you refer to me as a 'ghost', then it's a myth. In my travels I've heard many rumors about some sort of 'super assassin' who came out of the old Soviet Union. An unstoppable killer that goes by the name, The Silver Wraith."

Logan shook his head, "Well that's wonderful, our day just keeps getting better."

"Who were those guys back there anyway, what did they want?" asked Martinez as they continued to trudge through the wet sewers.

"They're after me, or more specifically, my cargo," said Xavier. "Unfortunately your team was in the wrong place at the wrong time. But now that you've become involved, they won't stop until you've been killed, you've seen too much to be allowed to live."

Minutes later a manhole cover behind an old, abandoned construction project slowly lifted and was slid aside. Xavier Greene, along with Martinez and Logan emerged behind the old, incomplete building. Xavier walked over to a blue tarp that was draped over the back of an old dumpster and pulled it aside to reveal the rusty Pinto he had picked up at the Citadel garage back in Atlanta. He opened the back hatch of the car and touched a few hidden buttons, causing several panels to open. In the larger of the two, he stashed his duffle bag, removing a few small items and putting them in his jacket pocket. In the smaller, heavily padded chamber he placed the virus' padded box. After closing the panels, Xavier opened yet another secret drawer.

"We're gonna need to be incognito, let me see what I've got in here, I should be able to come up with something," said Xavier as he started rummaging through the clothing in the drawer.

Suddenly, Logan drew his gun and pointed at Xavier, "I think you're forgetting what I was sent here to do."

Martinez looked back and forth between Logan and Xavier, "Bill are you crazy? He just saved our lives."

"And because of that fact, I'll let him walk. But the virus is coming with us," said Logan as he continued to hold Xavier in his sights.

Xavier sighed, "While I admire your dedication Agent, the fact remains that we have larger problems at the moment. Need I remind you, time is of the essence. If those soldiers, or especially the Silver Wraith, find us, we're as good as dead. We're both outnumbered and outgunned. Because of that fact, we need to get under cover and on the road, we'll sort out semantics later." Xavier turned and looked at Logan. Logan returned his stare for what seemed like an eternity before he uncocked his gun and returned to his shoulder holster. Xavier smiled briefly and threw Logan a change of clothes. In the meantime, Xavier slipped on a pair of padded coveralls and a cap. He then rubbed some tinted lotion on his face and fastened on a very realistic looking mustache.

He turned to Logan and Martinez and asked "How do I look?" They were stunned. Gone was the skeletally thin assassin with the pale skin and faintly European accent. In his place was a slightly dumpy, weather and sun beaten, middle aged man with a matching southwestern accent. In the meantime, Logan had switched into a black t-shirt, ball cap and sunglasses. Xavier rummaged through the clothing again before turning to Martinez.

"I'm sorry, but I'm afraid I didn't pack any clothes for a lady." Martinez pointed to a brown ball cap and Xavier threw it to her.

"It's alright, I've got this handled," said Martinez as she whipped off her bulletproof vest and navy blouse to reveal a white, tight fitting tank top underneath. She pulled her hair up in a ponytail and tucked it through the back of the hat and put on her sunglasses.

Xavier raised his eyebrows, "You'll have to sit in the back and stay low, as the purpose of this exercise is to blend in, not attract more attention."

Martinez grinned big as she opened the door of the Pinto and threw her vest in the back. "I'll take that as a compliment, now let's get going."

Logan climbed in the passenger door and stashed his gun under the front seat. Xavier climbed in the driver's door and started the engine. He turned to the two agents, "One last thing, turn off both of your cellphones. At this point we don't know who to trust, and the last thing I need is someone, whether it be your employer or theirs, tracking our movements."

Xavier slowly pulled the car out into traffic and started down the street at a leisurely pace. "The trick," Xavier started, "is to blend in. To every outside appearance, we're just ordinary people. If we see one of the soldiers walking down the street, don't even give him a sideways glance, pay him no mind. If he realizes you recognize him, it'll give us away."

They rode in silence for a few blocks and as they did, they passed one of the soldiers on the street. He wasn't carrying his machine gun or wearing his helmet but he was clearly wearing the same black outfit. He didn't give the Pinto a second glance as they drove past. After a minute or so, everyone seemed to relax a little. Finally Logan broke the silence.

"Thanks again for saving our lives back there, you could've left us to fend for ourselves and you didn't. That means a lot."

"As I've said before Agent Logan," responded Xavier, "you're just doing your job. Besides, I may yet need your help."

"Now let's not get carried away," countered Logan, "just because I appreciate what you've done for us, doesn't mean that I'm just forgetting about my duty. At this point, I'm fine with you going your separate way, but I still plan on taking the virus back to my superiors, a mission is a mission and I'm not just gonna walk away from that."

Xavier narrowed his eyes and seemed to focus entirely on driving as the car moved on in silence for several minutes. At a stop light they came to a halt in front of an electronics store with a large TV in the front window.

Suddenly Martinez erupted from the backseat, "Son of a bitch, Logan check it out!" she said as she pointed toward the TV. One of the national news channels was showing breaking news and there on the TV were Logan and Martinez' pictures with the headline 'BIOTERROR PLOT UNCOVERED'. The ticker running under the story went on to explain that FBI agents Logan and Martinez are suspected of working with an international bio-terrorist. Logan sat slack jawed staring at the screen as the light turned green and Xavier pulled calmly away from the intersection. He glanced over at Logan, "Still think you have a mission to accomplish?"

Logan slammed his hands on the dashboard, "Goddamnit, this is ridiculous! That does it, I've got to call in and set things straight." He fumbled with his pocket until he finally got the cellphone out. Xavier smacked the phone out of his hand before he could turn it on.

"What the hell are you doing?" yelled Logan, as Xavier continued to calmly drive along.

"The question is, what the hell are you doing? They think you're a bio-terrorist, at least that's what everyone is being told, and you want to turn on the one way they have of tracking you?" Xavier shook his head, "Don't be a fool Agent Logan, you're being played. Powerful forces are at work here. They're the ones who created the news story, and they're the ones that I'm pretty certain your bosses answer to. If you turn on that phone, we're doomed and the mission is doomed. At this point, your best chance is to stick with me and help me complete my mission. With any luck it can all be sorted out once the virus is out of play for good."

Logan sat for a long while looking out the window before turning to look at Martinez for a few moments. Finally he shrugged his shoulders. "What choice do we have? Okay fine, we'll do it your way. At this point I'm probably gonna end up dead or hidden away in some CIA black ops prison, so what do I have to lose? Are you in Martinez? Wanna help stick it to the man?"

"If it hurts whoever put up that story on the TV, I'm all for it," said Martinez, "although at this point, I'm not feeling like we have much of a chance. What's our move, Xavier?"

"Luckily I already have a plan in place," started Xavier as he glanced in his rearview, "this whole time I've been in a holding pattern, waiting on a delivery. This allowed the Brotherhood to catch up with me, as well as your team and the army of mercenaries that we encountered back at the warehouse. Hopefully our wait is almost up and we'll be able to move forward with the rest of the mission before they figure out what my plan is. In the meantime, I'm going to stop and check on my delivery before bringing you as up to speed on everything as I can."

Xavier pulled into the back of the parking lot of a bustling shopping center and pulled out a prepaid cellphone he had purchased at the truck stop that morning. As Martinez and Logan looked on, Xavier dialed a number and waited for a tone. Once he got the tone he punched in a three digit code and hung up. The trio sat in silence for almost a minute before the phone started to ring.

"Stephen, have you made any progress?" said Xavier as he answered the phone.

"I was beginning to think you weren't gonna call," replied Stephen. "You'll be pleased to know that you're now set up in the system at the Hastings Biotech Facility with full administrative privileges. I've express mailed the package to Tommy's Place, a bar that is on the outskirts of town on the highway to the facility. I put 'Care of Xavier Greene' on it."

"That's excellent!" exclaimed Xavier.

"Don't be too quick to pat me on the back," continued Stephen. "The facility has been undergoing maintenance on the computer systems and I was able to inject a code into it that will make you an administrator. Unfortunately the crew doing the onsite maintenance won't leave until about 8am tomorrow, so you can't access the lab until tomorrow morning at the earliest."

This troubled Xavier because the longer this drew out, the more the likelihood that their pursuers would figure out what his true intentions were. If the mercenaries got to the lab first and waited on them, they would be finished.

"Well you've still done excellent work. I appreciate the effort and I'll arrange for you to be paid in our usual manner. In the meantime, please keep pursuing the money trail for me. We've got to get that sorted out."

"Sure thing Xavier," came the reply from Stephen. "Be careful and try to stay alive, sounds like you have a real pressure cooker going on out there." Then the phone went dead.

"Who was that?" asked Logan after they had sat in silence for a few moments longer than he cared for.

"A friend," replied Xavier. "And we have good news for a change. The package I've been expecting will be delivered within the next three hours to a bar not far from here. Unfortunately we won't be able to access the facility until tomorrow morning due to some complications."

"At last, something appears to be going our way," said Martinez as she shifted positions trying to get comfortable in the backseat of the pinto.

"Yes but it appears we have a few hours to kill," said Xavier. "Why don't we find somewhere to get something to eat? We're going to need our strength and the last time we tried to eat together, we never succeeded. What do you say?"

Logan chuckled. "Okay, you have a deal, as long as you promise not to order soup."

Xavier's face lifted into an amused grin, "Okay, you have yourself a deal."

CHAPTER EIGHTEEN

Tommy's Place

Forty five minutes later, the trio sat, still incognito, in the back booth of a typical roadside restaurant. Logan had ordered a beer to help ease his nerves, while Xavier and Martinez had gotten water. After mulling over the menu and ordering their food, Logan made a gesture towards Xavier.

"Come on, spill it," he said. "You said you were gonna explain what was going on and why were now fugitives from justice with you, so let's hear it, I'm all ears."

Xavier sat looking out at the neon signs on the roadway, as if contemplating the best way to explain the delicate situation that they found themselves in. Finally he sighed and looked across the table at his two co-conspirators.

"As promised, I will brief you on as much of this as I can, I'll have to leave certain details out, but I'm sure you understand?"

Logan nodded and Xavier continued on, filling them in on what the virus was and how it had come into his possession, conveniently leaving out any mention of the Citadel by name, or his insubordination. He then briefly outlined his plan for destroying it.

"But what I don't understand is," started Martinez. "Why us? Why do you need our help to complete the mission? Why doesn't your 'employer' just send backup?"

Xavier sat for a moment as if contemplating the best way to answer, "That simply isn't possible. The people who are pursuing us are powerful people. They have vast resources and they are willing to do anything to get this virus. I'm assuming it's to be used as leverage, or who knows, maybe weaponized somehow. In either case, if this virus were released, accidentally or on purpose, it would cause a massive extinction level event. I can't allow it to fall into the wrong hands. It simply must be destroyed and it's up to us alone to do it."

Logan shook his head, "Wait, wait, you're telling me that in addition to being on the run from the FBI, we're also being hunted by some type of multinational cabal type group that is now sending goons like the ones we just fought after us? And to top it off, we have no backup? Jesus, what a suicide mission!"

Xavier leveled his gaze at Logan, "No, I'm telling you that your government is being used in conjunction with the team of mercenaries to try to get their hands on this virus. The people you work for are compromised, I promise you. They are simply a tool that is being used to try to ratchet up more pressure on us. They created that smear campaign against you two as well. However I'm hoping if we complete the mission and destroy the virus, then my employer will be able to help straighten up any damage done to your reputation and get everything smoothed out."

"And if you're wrong?" asked Martinez, leaning in close.

Xavier sat for a moment before returning her gaze, "Then we're as good as dead."

"I'm still trying to come to grips with this whole thing. You mean to tell me that they have people embedded in the FBI and the US Government?" said Logan as he took another drink from his pint.

"No, I'm telling you that the FBI answers to them. They call the shots, and are more powerful than any one country." Xavier stopped and glanced down at his watch. "I've said too much. Trust me, the less you know about the people we are up against, the better. I promise you, we'll get all this straightened out once the virus is destroyed."

They ate in silence for a few moments before Logan spoke up again, "So if you can't tell us about these people who are pursuing us and manipulating everything against us, what can you tell me about whomever employs you? I mean, obviously the people you work for have connections, from the sounds of it you've been pursuing this Brotherhood all over the world, but now suddenly you're on your own? What gives."

Logan waited for an answer as Xavier ate his food without looking up. After a few moments he glanced at his watch again and pulled out a wad of bills that he dropped on the table. "Time to go, our package awaits."

He then got up and walked away from the booth leaving Logan and

Martinez sitting.

"What a piece of work," said Logan as he looked at Martinez. "I wonder if we would have been better off turning ourselves in."

They caught up with Xavier in the parking lot of the restaurant, which just happened to be right beside Tommy's Place. The glow of the large neon sign with the caricature of an American Indian chief cast a strange hue on the parking lot. Loud music blared from Tommy's Place and a large number of motorcycles were parked out front.

Logan whistled through his teeth, "Man, this sure ain't no tourist trap, what's the plan?"

Xavier glanced up at him briefly, before going back to shuffling through his things in the back of the car. "The plan is that you two will stay here and I'll go in and retrieve the package. The less attention we attract, the better."

"If you say so," said Martinez. "But how will we know if you need help?"

Xavier turned and looked at Martinez, "Let's hope it doesn't come to that, but if it does, I'm sure it will be obvious."

With that Xavier turned and walked briskly over to Tommy's Place. The inside smelled of stale beer and cigarette smoke. The old, dark wooden walls were littered with neon beer signs that doubled as most of the lighting. Xavier made his way around the dark, noisy room to the bar area. Sitting down at a bar stool he asked the bartender for Tommy. The bartender looked at him with a puzzled look before shrugging and pointing to the end of the bar. There Xavier saw a man who appeared to be nearly 7 feet tall, with shoulder length black hair. The man's face looked weathered and rough and bore the scars of what must have been hundreds of bar fights. Xavier tipped the bartender and walked to the end of the bar.

"Pardon me," said Xavier as he approached the large man. He turned and looked at Xavier with two black eyes set into slits in his face. The stare he gave Xavier was impossible to read, the battle scarred face stoic, with a scowl that seemed to convey threats without a single word spoken. Slowly he stood up, towering over Xavier.

"What can I do for you?" he asked, his voice a low rumble.

"Well, I'm looking for Tommy," replied Xavier, looking up at the imposing figure before him.

"You found him. Now like I said, what can I do for you?" replied the large man, obviously getting impatient.

Xavier looked at the man matter of factly, "I believe you have a package for me, my name is Xavier Greene."

At this the expression on the man's face turned dark and a vein bulged out in the side of his neck. He made a small gesture with his hand and suddenly Xavier was surrounded by four huge men.

Tommy reached behind the bar and pulled out a small package with his massive hand.

"You've got a lot of nerve little man. You think I'm some kinda damn errand boy? You think you can just have stuff delivered here? What else do you want? Want me to do your fucking laundry? You little clown. Well I'll tell you what, I got your package, and I've decided that it's COD and my boys here are gonna help me collect. It'll help ease my shame for being treated like a punk."

A sinister grin spread across Tommy's face as the four huge men closed ranks around Xavier. Ignoring the impending peril, Xavier spoke up.

"Oh, I believe you misunderstand me. Despite my appearance, I'm a business man and had no intention of not compensating you for your services." With that he removed a huge wad of bills from his pocket and tossed it to the large man. Tommy caught the wad and thumbed through it. He stopped counting at five thousand and put the wad of bills in his jacket pocket.

"I hope that more than makes up for any inconvenience, or misunderstanding," said Xavier as Tommy waved off the men and slid the package down the counter to him.

"Tell you what," said Tommy, as he patted the large wad of cash in his jacket pocket. "Feel free to have things dropped off here anytime. But next time, give me a head's up first. Now get out of here, and have yourself a good fucking night."

Xavier quickly slipped out of the bar before Tommy changed his mind. Once in the parking lot, he pulled out a handkerchief and started wiping the makeup off his face. He also pulled off the false mustache and cap. By the time he reached the pinto, he unzipped the coveralls and stepped out of them to reveal his normal suit underneath. Back to looking like himself, Xavier took out a small knife and opened the package. He pulled out the security lanyard and the paper with the security codes and stuck them in his pocket. A brief glance of the schematics revealed the incinerator was in one of the sublevels of the facility. He folded the schematics up and put them in his jacket as well before getting back into the car.

"Well that seemed to go well," said Martinez as Xavier fastened his safety belt and started the car.

"Tommy was the consummate businessman," replied Xavier. "As I had hoped. I just had to make it worth his while. Now we have the credentials to get in, we just have to wait for the maintenance crew to leave. In the meantime, we should find a place to lay low and get some rest, we're going to need it."

CHAPTER NINETEEN

Race to the Laboratory

The sun shone behind a series of breaking clouds, giving them orange and purple hues out over the barren landscape. A lone car rolled down the highway, a dirty brown pinto with rust spots coming out of the wheel wells. It had been a fitful night, the anticipation of the mission didn't leave much room for restful sleep, coupled with the fact that Xavier still didn't know if he could completely trust his two companions. They had taken turns watching out while the other two tried to sleep, but Xavier had never let his guard down. He knew this was the most dangerous part of the mission, as long as they were in the town, they could blend in, but here on the long, desolate road to the lab, they were exposed. If their play had been figured out, they were done. Then Martinez spoke up from the backseat.

"Look, back on the horizon. I can barely make it out, but it looks like a black helicopter heading our way."

Xavier looked in the rearview and pivoted the mirror around until he found it. As he watched the sinister black shape grow in his mirror, he knew they had been found. If they managed to stop them before they reached the lab, all was lost. Ahead Xavier saw the dirt road that led to the facility. He slowed and turned off, never taking his eyes off the ever approaching helicopter.

"You know we're sitting ducks right?" asked Logan.

Xavier nodded, "We're not finished yet, whereas the Brotherhood wanted to unleash the virus on the world, these mercenaries have a different mission. They need the virus intact, so I doubt they'll use lethal force. Hopefully we can find some way to use that to our advantage."

Just then a hail of bullets raked the ground just inches from them, slinging dirt clods all over the car. Xavier barely swerved and continued down the path.

"Are you sure about your theory?" yelled Logan as another volley of bullets rained down around the car.

"Absolutely," replied Xavier as he dodged chunks of dirt. "They're just trying to frighten us. We have to keep going, they won't risk a direct hit on the car. If we stop out here in the open we're finished."

The helicopter swung back around for another pass, but this time instead of firing, they swooped in low and hovered just above the car, creating a huge dust storm. Xavier swerved back and forth, barely able to see the road from the dust stirred up by the helicopter. Twice the car threatened to fishtail but Xavier somehow held on, abruptly the helicopter pulled back up to avoid a patch of scrub trees that lined a small section of the road. Xavier looked ahead, after the small patch of trees there was nothing but open ground. If the helicopter swooped in close like that again he would have a hard time keeping control of the car.

"This is crazy, we're never gonna make it," said Martinez as she looked at the vast expanse before them. "Even if you manage to keep control, the dust they stir up could end up causing the car to choke out. If the engine dies we're goners."

Xavier nodded his head, "Agreed, but we don't have much choice, if either of you have any ideas, I'm open to suggestions."

"I might have an idea," said Logan as they neared the end of the patch of trees. "Can you pull a 'doughnut' in this thing?"

"I'm afraid I'm not familiar with that terminology. What's a 'doughnut'?" asked Xavier.

Logan pulled out his gun and checked the chamber, "It's where you turn the wheel sharply and floor it, causing the car to spin round and round."

"I think I can handle that," replied Xavier. "But how does that figure in?"

Logan rolled down his window, "No time to explain, just be ready on my signal."

Xavier nodded as they shot out from under the expanse of trees. The helicopter immediately reappeared and opened fire. Bullets streaked past the car but left it untouched. The helicopter circled around and started bearing down on the car again. Just as they swooped in low, Logan yelled "NOW!"

Xavier immediately turned the wheel and floored it, causing the Pinto to whip around in tight circles, stirring up a huge column of dust that engulfed the helicopter, coating it's windshield threatening to clog it's vents. The engine sputtered as the pilot struggled in his attempt to pull away from the expanding column. Just then, the car whipped to a stop and Logan leveled his .357 at the window of the cockpit. He squeezed off two shots that appeared to hit the dead center of the driver's window. Suddenly, the helicopter began to lurch uncontrollable through the sky, spiraling around before slamming into the side of a large rock outcropping.

"Great shot agent!" said Xavier as he watched the smoldering wreckage slide down the rocks before coming to a rest at the bottom of the mesa. It settled to a halt and a column of smoke poured out of it.

"We're not out of the woods yet, look!" said Martinez, pointing as a door was shoved off the side of the wreckage. Several men crawled out, followed by the tall, mesh clad form of the Silver Wraith. Xavier spun the car back toward the path and drove on, following it around a large rock outcropping. Behind it they saw a small, state of the art facility lined with solar panels and surrounded by a chain link fence.

"This tiny place is where we're heading?" asked Logan

"Most of the facility is underground," replied Xavier. "What we're seeing is just the tip of the iceberg, so to speak."

Instead of going through the front gate, Xavier turned the car and started driving around the perimeter.

"Where the hell are you going? The front door is that way!" said Martinez as they tried to brace themselves across the bumpy terrain.

"Yes, but I want the car out of sight, in case we survive and need to slip away unseen," replied Xavier as he fought to keep control as the Pinto bounced across the landscape.

Moments later they had parked the Pinto in a crevice of the large outcropping that seemed to cradle the facility within its curvature. The trio exited the car and Xavier made his way to the rear hatch, which he opened, along with several more secret panels that Logan and Martinez hadn't noticed before. With the greatest care, Xavier removed the small box containing the virus from it's padded holding area and tucked it in his jacket. He also removed a large duffle bag, which he handed to Logan.

"Jeez, what have you got in here, bricks?" asked Logan, as he sat the bag on the ground and unzipped it. Inside he found a variety of both handguns and small machine guns as well as ammo.

"Whoa, you've been holding back on us this whole time. And here I thought you were more of a knife guy," remarked Martinez as she grabbed an extra sidearm and a UZI from the bag.

"I'm for whatever tool is the most practical at the time," remarked Xavier as he finished packing away several small packages in his jacket. "Let's get going, we don't have much time."

The trio traversed the short area between the large mesa and the facility and found a spot where the rain had rutted out the ground under the fence. The slipped easily through the opening under the fence and quickly sprinted across the facility grounds, past large solar panels and nondescript metal buildings, no doubt housing the ventilation systems. As they rounded the corner to make their way to the main entrance, an unwelcome sight greeted them. Off in the distance, beyond the front gate was a small group of mercenaries with the Silver Wraith in the lead.

"Oh, just great," said Logan as he raised his weapon to fire.

"Don't bother," said Xavier. They're way out of range. We just need to get inside and get set up."

As they approached the front door they noticed a large chain and padlock fastening the front door.

"Keep an eye on our friends," said Xavier as he felt the weight of the padlock in his hand while reaching into his jacket with the other hand.

"Can you pick it that fast?" asked Martinez as she eyed the mercenaries drawing ever closer.

Without answering Xavier pulled a small spray can from his jacket pocket. It had a slender straw that he inserted into the padlock and pressing down on the cap, gave it a spray. Instantly the lock began fizzing and sputtering, before it finally fell apart. Xavier removed the chain from the door and swiped his security card. Stephen hadn't let him down, the light flashed green and the door opened. Xavier placed the can back in his jacket and smiled at Martinez.

"Practicality," he said as he ushered them in the door.

Inside was a small reception room with a call center desk in the center of it. Xavier stopped at the control desk and punched in a code from a piece of paper he had in his pocket. Once the first code was accepted, he punched in the second code and the lights suddenly came on.

"There, the facility is fully operational, the incinerator should be online," said Xavier as the trio moved past the desk and with another swipe of Xavier's card, proceeded down a small stairway which led to what appeared to be a lab. Steel tables lined the far side of the room.

"This would be a perfect choke point. If we use those large tables for cover we could pin them in the stairwell," said Agent Logan as he started for one of the tables.

"Excellent plan Agent," said Xavier. "If the two of you can hold them in that door way long enough for me to take the elevator down to the incinerator, this should be over before we know it."

"Right, then all we have to do is get back out, past a gang of trained mercenaries and some sort of super assassin," said Martinez as she helped Logan move a couple of the heavy lab tables together to form their cover.

"We'll cross that bridge when we come to it," said Xavier as he swiped his card to open the elevator. "Good luck," and with that he disappeared into the elevator and the only sound was the hum of the computers and the smooth hiss of the ventilation system.

CHAPTER TWENTY

Stand off

The room was quiet, only disturbed by the sounds of Martinez and Logan arranging their weapons behind their makeshift cover. Fluorescent lights cast a bright glow on the metal and tile room, giving an overly, though entirely appropriate, feeling of sterility to the environment. Logan kept a watchful eye on the stairwell as he went from gun to gun, checking the magazines. When he was satisfied that everything was in order, he settled in with his weapon cocked, waiting on the team of mercenaries to come down the stairs. Martinez finally broke the silence.

"Definitely not what I pictured myself doing when I got up yesterday morning," she said as she trained the sight of her gun on the doorway.

Logan nodded, "No kidding, at this point I would rather be sitting at my desk playing solitaire."

"How long till you figure they'll show up?" asked Martinez.

He shrugged, "Hard to tell, they're definitely playing it safe. They have to know we saw them approaching the gate. Of course I figured they don't have the luxury of having their own keycard to get in so they may be trying to jimmy the door."

Just then they heard a muffled sound from up the stairwell. Martinez and Logan tensed, knowing that before long their silent interlude would dissolve into pure chaos. Just then, they heard the beep from the keypad at the top of the steps as the tumblers released, opening the door to the stairs.

Logan glanced at Martinez, "What the hell? They have a keycard?"

The sounds of footsteps echoed through the eerily silent room.

Logan and Martinez watched as a couple of the mercenaries crept into view. Their fingers tensed on the triggers as they watched them creep cautiously down the stairs. Just as the first of the soldiers stepped into the room, the agents opened fire. Instantly the first two mercenaries dropped to the floor in a heap. The rest of the mercenaries, having no cover they could safely reach, scrambled back up the stairs and out of sight. The room was silent again, the smell of small arms fire ripe in the air.

The silence stretched on, except for the muffled sounds of the mercenaries regrouping at the top of the stairs. Logan and Martinez watched for signs of life in the two mercenaries that had been hit. One stared lifelessly up at the ceiling, the other had fallen back, it's body slumped against the wall, blood streaming from under his helmet. Logan glanced at Martinez and motioned to keep the guns trained on the stairs.

"So far, so good," said Logan, as he readjusted his grip on his AR-15.

Suddenly, without warning, the Silver Wraith bounded down the stairs, a machine gun under each arm. Logan and Martinez opened fire again when the Wraith hit the bottom step but they underestimated it's agility. It effortlessly ducked and rolled forward, away from their barrage and returned fire with both guns. Bullets ripped at the makeshift cover and the pair were forced to crouch down behind it in the face of the onslaught. With Logan and Martinez pinned down, the other mercenaries quickly ran down the steps and slid behind some large coolers and cabinets that were located on the opposite side of the room. The Wraith emptied both guns, tossed them aside, and signaled for one of the mercenaries to throw it another. Just as it turned to catch the new gun, Logan whipped around the end of the table and fired at the Wraith with his .357. The shot hit it in the shoulder, spinning it full circle. The other mercenaries opened fire however, and Logan quickly found himself pinned down behind the table. The Wraith regained its footing, grabbed its gun, and charged across the room towards the tables. Startled by the Wraith running into the line of fire, the mercenaries were forced to stop firing, so as not to hit the Wraith by accident. As the firing ceased, Logan lunged toward the corner of the table, preparing to fire again but, to his shock and surprise, the Wraith was already there. Without hesitation, it kicked him in the face, sending him backwards across the floor, slamming into Martinez. Logan spit blood as he scrambled off his back and raised his gun toward the Wraith, who already had it's gun trained on him.

"If we're going, it ain't without a fight!" said Martinez as she scrambled into a seated position, her gun also trained on the Wraith.

Strangely, the Wraith made no move, other than tilting its head, as if accessing the situation. The tense standoff stretched out for several moments. Neither the Wraith or the agents made a move. The mercenaries started to get up from behind their defenses, but the Wraith held up it's hand, signaling them to stay where they were. Looking back and forth between the agents and the mercenaries, the Wraith suddenly pulled a keycard from a hidden pocket, swiped it, and pushed the elevator button. As the door opened, the Wraith dropped it's gun and entered the elevator. The door slid shut and the lights above the door showed it descending toward the sub levels.

"What the hell?" asked Martinez as Logan scrambled back up to his knees and swiped the blood off his chin.

"I have no idea," he replied, as he leveled his gun at the mercenaries, causing them to duck down behind the coolers. "But at least temporarily, I think we're the luckiest people on Earth, even though I wish we had a way to warn Xavier of what was coming."

CHAPTER TWENTY-ONE

So Close...

The bottom level of the lab was quiet except for the muted sound of the air vents and the hum of the fluorescent lights. Xavier exited the elevator and approached the central workstation. The facility was state of the art and had been designed to run with as few people as possible, therefore each floor had a central workstation that controlled all the lab functions for that particular level. Xavier took a few seconds to familiarize himself with the control panel as it was booting up. After consulting his notes, he typed in the command to bring the incinerator online. After a few seconds, the computer asked for his security clearance code and Xavier once again glanced through his notes and typed in the code. Instantly the lights in the main lab came on and a low hum could be heard, as if something was powering up. Xavier locked the computer terminal so that it couldn't be tampered with and headed into the main lab.

The lab was a large, long room filled with workstations and computers, with a ceiling lined with a network of pipes and a higher section in the middle. Xavier made his way past the various computers and workstations, all spotless, despite having not been used in over a year. At the far end of the room, stood the incinerator. The device took up most of the far wall and consisted of a touchscreen control panel, a series of buttons, a small glass door and a lever to fire the incinerator.

Xavier approached the touchscreen and entered his security code. The incinerator's hum picked up in intensity as the burners came online. A few moments later, the touchscreen directed him to place the virus in the incinerator chamber. With the utmost care, Xavier reached in his pocket and pulled out the ominous padded case that had been the cause of so much trouble. After unfastening the clasp on the container, Xavier slowly pulled out the small vial of cloudy white liquid. He held it up to the light, looking at the swirling, almost milky, white liquid contained inside. He marveled at how such a small, seemingly insignificant thing could hold so much sway over the world. Because of this small vial of liquid, dozens had died, chaos had been unleashed around the world, and powerful groups had moved heaven and earth to get it at all cost.

"But enough of this," he thought as he reached over and unlocked the thick glass door. It was time to put this to rest once and for all. Ever so delicately, he placed the vial into the center of the chamber and carefully adjusted the grips to hold it in place. After closing the door and locking it, Xavier moved back to the touch screen, where he set the temperature of the incinerator to maximum. After accepting the command, the touch screen prompted him that the incinerator was ready. Xavier glanced at the virus one last time and thought about how glad he would be to rid himself of this albatross. He punched the button to prime the burner and reached for the lever that would activate the incinerator and obliterate the virus forever.

Just as he gripped the lever and started to pull it down, a dagger smashed into the console just below his hand. Sparks erupted everywhere as Xavier recoiled and spun to see where the dagger had come from. Across the room, standing just inside the door was the Silver Wraith. Xavier felt himself breaking out in a cold sweat as he tried to figure out how the Wraith had gotten into the room without detection. Had he been so obsessed and focused on the virus that he didn't hear the Wraith enter the room? Had he let his guard down while focusing on setting up the incinerator, or was the Wraith just that good? He glanced back over his shoulder at the dagger that was still stuck in the smoldering panel, and another question seemed to push the others out of the way. Why was he still alive? An assassin of the Wraith's stature could have just as easily put the dagger in the base of his skull, why hit the panel instead?

As if anticipating his question, the Wraith took a step forward, reached behind it's back and pulled out it's two curved swords. It spun the blades twice and took several steps forward. Xavier felt his blood go cold. Of course, it all made sense now, the Wraith had seen his katana back at the warehouse. It felt it had the mission in hand, and now it was curious. It wanted to test Xavier's proficiency with his sword, one on one with no interference. He wondered what had become of the two agents he had left upstairs? If the Wraith was here, what did that say about their chances? Was he the only one left? But just as puzzling, where were the rest of the mercenaries that he had seen with it?

The Wraith tilted its head slightly, as if growing slightly impatient with him. The questions would have to wait. He was alive for now, and with the Wraith wanting to prolong this into a duel, he would have to figure out how to use this to his advantage. Slowly Xavier reached under his jacket, expanded the hilt of the katana and pulled it from its scabbard. The Wraith spun its blades again in anticipation as it walked out toward the middle of the large lab. It crouched slightly and assumed a battle stance that Xavier wasn't familiar with. Xavier also started to move deliberately toward the center of the room, where they circled each other slowly as Xavier switched in and out of various kata positions. Each time he would change the Wraith would change to a corresponding position. Xavier observed each of the Wraith's different stances and compared them to the katas that he was taking on. By reflecting on the openings in his stances, he was hoping he could compare that to the Wraith's corresponding stances and figure out what the strengths of each one were. Of course, he couldn't be exactly sure what the stances meant, for example was it countering his strong stance with a quick stance, or a strong stance of its own? As they continued their dance of death, he felt his pulse starting to rise. Despite his best efforts, the adrenaline started to flow as he continued this initial chess match with this mythical, lethal predator. This was but a prelude, a sizing up of each other before the real game began. The myth of the indestructible assassin was about to get tested with the fate of the world hanging in the balance...

CHAPTER TWENTY-TWO
Dwindling Advantage

Several floors above, the room had exploded into chaos. Logan and Martinez had pinned the group of mercenaries down by relentlessly attacking, while they were still stunned by the Wraith's sudden disappearance. But that had lasted only a few, short minutes before the mercenaries had regrouped and focused their superior firepower on the federal agent's makeshift shelter.

Logan slapped in a fresh clip and grimaced as another wave of weapon fire ricocheted off of the steel tables that were serving as their shelter. "You ever had one of those days when you wished you had called in sick?" he said with a grin.

Martinez shook her head and returned fire through a small gap in the tables. "What? This isn't your idea of a good time? Don't tell me 'Wild Bill' is going soft on me?"

Another wave of gunfire swept across the tables. "Nah it's not that, it's just that I'm starting to get a sinking feeling that we're not walking away from this. These guys have us pinned down and that's bad enough. Sooner or later we run out of ammo and then what?" They ducked as another wave of automatic weapon fire blasted the wall behind them. "But even if we do hold them off, we don't even know if Xavier will be able to succeed. I mean, he's very good at what he does, but the Wraith is down there and for all we know he's dead and any minute now that silver kook is gonna come flying out the elevator and decapitate us. I just don't see many good ways out of this."

Suddenly an even heavier wave of gunfire erupted and Martinez and Logan ducked down as shrapnel from the table and the wall scattered around them. Out of the corner of her eye Martinez swore she saw movement. Suddenly the gunfire ceased and all was silent, except for the hiss of the air-conditioning system. Martinez peered through the gap in the table but saw nothing.

"Something's up, I swore I just saw movement in the reflection of those cabinet doors," said Martinez as she wearily scanned the room. The thick haze of gun smoke hung over the room and she could see the cabinets that the mercenaries were hiding behind, but something caught her eye to the left. On the far side of the room she saw movement and sure enough, there were two of the mercenaries hiding behind the first row of shelves. There were four sections on the far side and Martinez suddenly realized that if the mercenaries made it to the fourth section they would catch herself and Logan in a flanking maneuver and they would have nowhere to hide. Before she could explain what was going on the volley of gunfire started again and they were pinned down.

Over the din of the gunfire Martinez yelled into Logan's ear, "We've got a serious problem, they are trying to flank us using the cover of the cabinets and cubbies on the far side of the room." Suddenly the gunfire ended leaving the last word of her sentence way too loud. Logan looked through the gap and saw the two men who had now made it to the second section.

"Oh shit, this is bad," said Logan as he scanned around them for a way to even the odds. They didn't have a clear shot at the men and with another volley or two they would have them. He had to think of something quick. Then he saw the supply cabinet behind them.

"I've got a plan, return fire and don't let up until I tell you!" said Logan, as Martinez opened fire indiscriminately through the gap in the table, Logan slid on his knees to the supply cabinet and pulled an oxygen tank out from under it. As Martinez continued laying down the cover fire he rolled it over to the left hand side of the table and began lining it up roughly with the section of shelves that the mercenaries were taking cover behind.

Martinez glanced over warily, "What the hell are you doing?" she asked as she continued to pelt the mercenaries' shelter with gunfire.

"Oh, you know, improvising," said Logan as he slammed the nozzle of the oxygen tank with the butt of his rifle. In an instant the oxygen tank roared to life, rocketing across the floor straight at the shelves. Logan took aim and opened fire on it with his rifle. Just as it reached the shelves the tank exploded into a huge ball of fire as Logan dove behind the table. The explosion was deafening and the fire ball expanded throughout the middle of the room, threatening to engulf them all. Logan and Martinez crouched behind their table as the fire billowed over the top of their shelter and across the ceiling. Just as suddenly as it started the fireball burnt itself out, and the room was left filled with a thick black smoke. The sound of glass breaking in the fire and coughing were the only sounds. Slowly, Logan and Martinez looked around the corner of their table. The shelves on the far side of the room had been completely destroyed, the burning remains of the two men could be seen amongst the rubble. Suddenly, the sprinkler systems came on, drenching the room and putting out the fires from the explosion.

Leaning against the charred table in the deluge of water, Martinez gave Logan a look and shook her head, "How about you warn me the next time you plan on 'improvising'."

Logan chuckled and adjusted his stetson, "You can doubt the methods, but you can't doubt the effectiveness." Martinez smiled in spite of herself, marveling at the insanity of her partner. Out of nowhere a round of gunfire pummeled their shelter, shearing off the corner of their makeshift shelter. Martinez and Logan dropped down and returned fire, but between bursts Logan caught a look from Martinez and instantly knew what she meant. It was going to take more than a miracle for them to make it out of there alive.

CHAPTER TWENTY-THREE

Battle against the Silver Wraith

The blade slashed through the air, missing Xavier's head by mere inches. Xavier blocked another slash with his katana and parried another, before dodging to narrowly avoid yet another slash. He had, quite frankly, never seen a style like this before and was having a great deal of trouble adapting to it. From the start of the battle he had found himself on the defensive, as the Wraith had displayed a savage, hyper aggressive style. It spun and swirled its blades, throwing itself head long at it's opponent with the reckless abandon of a viking berserker. During all this, Xavier had noticed that the Wraith did very little to protect itself. In fact, most of its attacks left it wide open to a counterstrike, but it moved with such ferocity and speed that he barely had time to plan a counter move, much less execute it.

A computer monitor erupted in sparks as the Wraith slashed through it. Xavier quickly moved around the desk, trying desperately to put some space between himself and his attacker. To his dismay, the Wraith hurdled the table and slashed at him with an overhead strike. Xavier blocked the strike and, as he predicted, the second strike came from left and he blocked that as well, but as he parried it to start his counterstrike, the Wraith suddenly spun out of the way and slashed at his leg. At the last second Xavier moved, but not before the curved blade grazed his leg, slicing a small gash in it. Xavier stumbled against the wall, leaving a trail of blood smeared on it. The sight of blood only seemed to intensify the Wraith's attack as it moved in again, launching a quick slash with it's right hand sword. Xavier blocked the strike, but to his surprise it changed up it's tactics and instead of attacking with the other sword, as had been it's habit so far, it parried his block and threw a backhanded slash at his head. At the last second Xavier dodged the strike, causing the Wraith's sword to stab into the wall, momentarily sticking. Seizing the opening, Xavier slashed the Wraith's arm full force, but to his shock, instead of cleaving the arm from its body, the strike merely bounced off the limb. Immediately the Wraith countered by slashing at Xavier with it's other blade, while simultaneously ripping it's other blade from the wall. The slash sliced across his upper arm, and he felt hot blood flow down the inside of his sleeve. In desperation, Xavier kicked an office chair into the path of the aggressor and moved backwards, trying to get some space between himself and this seemingly invincible opponent. The Wraith merely kicked the chair out of the way before looking at Xavier and cocking its head at an angle as if closely observing its prey. It then shook its head and shrugged it's shoulders at Xavier, mocking him.

"I've got to cool down," Xavier thought. "I can't let it get under my skin, it has to have a weakness." Xavier continued to play up his injuries, hoping it would help him stall for time while he thought his way through this. Slowly, he limped backwards along the counters and grasped his slashed arm with his other arm. The ruse appeared to work, as the Wraith followed him slowly, but seemed content to soak in the moment, believing that the end of the fight was imminent. It stalked him along the side of the room, casually sweeping a chair out of the way with it's foot. It twirled one of it's blades menacingly but made no move to strike, anticipating that the end was near for its prey.

"It appears extremely reckless and doesn't seem to be worried about protecting itself at all. This ability allows it to attack with an unmatched fury because it doesn't seem to care about taking damage to itself. But the armor has to have a weak spot somewhere..." Suddenly Xavier's thoughts were cut off as it attacked again, spinning it's swords wildly and coming in with an overhead slash.

"Perfect" thought Xavier as he blocked the blow and the secondary blow that he knew would follow it. He swept both the swords together and spun out of the way, drawing his blade out from under them and in one constant motion, used his own spin to generate torque for a massive strike to the open midsection of the Wraith. The blow struck perfectly, catching it totally off guard and right in the middle of the abdomen. It was a total death strike, normally capable of cutting an opponent nearly in half, but to Xavier's horror the sword merely drug across it's midsection, leaving a trail of sparks and bounced off, unable to penetrate the mesh armor of the Wraith's suit. Seemingly embarrassed for being out-maneuvered, the Wraith suddenly slashed down at Xavier's head. Sheer reflexes allowed him to move out of the way at the last second and the blow instead cleaved off the corner of a desk as he slid past it. Xavier spun to counter the Wraith, but it slid around him with inhuman speed and slashed again, this time grazing his shoulder. Xavier winced in pain from the blow and stumbled over an overturned chair, hitting the floor only briefly before rolling back to his feet, expecting the onslaught to continue. To his surprise, the Wraith was seemingly over it's temporary tantrum and was now back to mocking him. It looked at him and patted it's stomach where his sword had bounced off harmlessly and shook its head.

Xavier backed away from the Wraith, giving himself some much needed space. How was he supposed to fight an enemy if he can't hurt it? His shoulder burned from the slash he had received, meanwhile his leg and arm stiffened from their wounds. He was losing blood, not enough to be lethal, but enough to eventually slow him down. That was a definite problem. He couldn't allow himself to slow down, because to not match the Wraith's breakneck pace would be certain death. However, he knew that wasn't sustainable either, as the Wraith could only maintain that pace because it was unconcerned with being struck with a counterattack. He had to find a way to make it vulnerable, that was his only chance. Perhaps if he was able to open up a vulnerability it would slow the Wraith down and force it to be a little more cautious. It was the only chance he had at this point, but he couldn't decide what seemed more impossible, finding a weakness, or staying alive.

CHAPTER TWENTY-FOUR

Status Update

Several floors above the gunfire was deafening. Moments earlier the sprinklers had finally stopped leaving the room drenched, the floors slick and everyone soaked to the bone. Reese shivered as he sat and stared at the radio the Wraith was supposed to take with it, lying on the floor amongst the growing pile of used shells. He shook his head and picked up the radio before slamming it down on the tile, shattering it into a million pieces.

"Dammit, what the hell are we supposed to do now?" He yelled to no one in particular. "The Wraith was supposed to kill those two idiots so we could all go downstairs and retrieve the virus from that other guy. Now we have no idea what's going on downstairs and thanks to that cowboy blowing up half the room we have no cover and no way to work our way across. Unless they run out of ammo, we're stuck."

Reese had found himself in charge of the squad sent out to retrieve the virus after their commanding officer, Bill Mikelson, was killed in the raid on the warehouse. After finally figuring out where the fugitives were heading, and despite losing the helicopter, he thought things had been going pretty good. In fact, if the Wraith had killed the two agents who were holed up on the other side of the room, like they had agreed upon, then they would have probably retrieved the virus by now and would be on their way. Instead, for reasons known only to itself, the Wraith had let them live, almost as a way to stall the rest of the team from getting to the lower level. He had no idea why it had decided to go it alone, it may have been part of a higher plan all along, perhaps they were all expendable as long as the Wraith got the virus. It was hard to tell, they had only been briefed on a need to know basis, and at this point he wished he hadn't jumped at the huge payday being offered. It had become apparent to him that huge paydays were easy to promise when most of them wouldn't make it back to cash in. He should have paid attention to the strange feeling he got when the Silver Wraith was added to their detail at the last minute. Something about it didn't seem right, but the money had been too good to turn down. Just then Malachi, his second in command, slid across the water covered floor and sat beside him, reloading his rifle as he did.

"What the hell are we supposed to do now? Sitting here and bouncing bullets off the wall while those two rats hide behind their shelter is getting old." Malachi said. "Why the hell didn't the Wraith drop those idiots?"

"I have no idea, but at least the sprinklers stopped," replied Reece. Malachi was younger than Reese by about four years and with his youth came impatience. "The Wraith's too independent. I didn't like it when we got saddled with it. Don't get me wrong, it's effective, but I doubt it has any loyalty or concern for us. At this point I don't think we have much choice but to try to wait those guys out, they're bound to run out of ammo before we do."

Malachi shook his head, "I would agree with you, but if you haven't noticed, they are barely firing back, just enough to get our guys to respond with long bursts. Whoever they are, they aren't dumb. They're playing us, causing us to expend a huge amount of ammo while they just hang back. I say we take things up a notch and get this wrapped up," he patted a grenade that was hanging off his belt and smiled. "What do you say Reese? Is it time to light it up?"

"Hell no, put that thing away!" snapped Reese. "You saw the oxygen tank that idiot flung across the room, don't you think there are more over there? You put a grenade in the wrong place and you'll blow the whole room off the map!"

"Yeah, good point. Sorry boss, I'm just getting antsy," replied Malachi. "Its just that since the rest of us aren't bullet proof, there's no way to get through there, and I don't know about you, but I'm more than ready to wrap this up."

"I agree," said Reese. "I wanted this to be an in and out, quick mission. We're not the only ones after this virus and the last thing we want is to get caught out here in the open."

Just then he felt the vibration of the cell phone he had tucked inside his kevlar vest. He opened the phone and checked the text message. "Well shit..." muttered Reese.

"What is it?" asked Malachi, trying to decipher the look on Reese's face.

"They want a progress report."

Malachi whistled through his teeth, "Well shit, indeed…"

CHAPTER TWENTY-FIVE

Unmasked

Xavier dodged a slash and managed to block the massive follow up attack that he had anticipated would come. As the battle continued, he had begun to learn the patterns and moves that the Wraith was using to the point he could almost anticipate it's attacks. That would have given him the advantage over a normal opponent. However, the Silver Wraith was hardly a normal opponent. With the knowledge that Xavier's katana couldn't pierce it's armor the Wraith pursued it's attacks with a reckless abandon like Xavier had never seen. It's pace was relentless as it stalked him around the lab. Twice Xavier had dodged attacks that would have cut him in half, only for a computer work station to bear the brunt of the assault and explode in a rain of sparks and glass that the Wraith barely acknowledged. Indeed, if the earlier assaults on Xavier had been the Wraith toying with it's potential victim, it was now bored and ready to finish the task at hand.

"I have to find a weakness," Xavier thought as he dodged another potentially fatal strike. He parried the follow up blow and launched a counter strike that caught the Wraith in the shoulder, but like the others, bounced off harmlessly as the Wraith continued it's unrelenting assault. Xavier rolled over a desk, barely dodging yet another strike by the Wraith, before moving backward down the row as the Wraith leaped over the desk and followed. Xavier desperately needed space and time to think. That was time he wasn't going to get, as the Wraith continued it's aggressive pursuit. He had to find a weakness or something to exploit that would give him an advantage, but what? The Wraith was supremely confident to the point of being reckless, indeed he had landed blows that would kill a normal person already, but with the Wraith being covered head to toe in some impenetrable armor, he hardly stood a chance.

Just then, the Wraith advanced on him again, closing the short distance between them in an instant. Thinking quickly, Xavier kicked a chair into the path of the Wraith, who easily jumped it, just like Xavier hoped it would. With the Wraith in midair, Xavier lunged and stabbed the center of the Wraith's chest. The blow of course had no effect except that it knocked the Wraith backwards and it landed flat on the floor. Xavier advanced on it, hoping to at least get it to drop one of it's crescent shaped swords. Instead, the Wraith, hardly seeming stunned, spun it's legs and tripped Xavier sending him careening into the side of a desk before hitting the floor. He quickly rolled into a crouch and at the last second dodged underneath a desk, avoiding a double downward slash by the Wraith that shattered the tile floor he had just occupied. Xavier rolled out the other side and kicked the desk, which flipped toward his opponent, hitting it in the hip and once again knocking it off balance. Xavier lunged and slashed the Wraith directly in the back of it's head, but once again the shot merely bounced off its head, as it responded with a sloppy counter slash of its own. Xavier easily dodged it and stepped back in to attack, but the Wraith kicked the table back up, and in Xavier's direction. The edge of the table slammed into his ribs and he stumbled backwards, once again dodging the Wraith's attack by inches. The Wraith hurdled the overturned desk and closed in on Xavier yet again. At the last second, Xavier swung straight up with his sword and slashed the support chain that held one side of a fluorescent light fixture. The fixture swung down and caught the Wraith in the face, causing an eruption of glass and sparks.

Xavier used the distraction to put some distance between himself and the Wraith, wishing he could somehow get enough separation to make it to the incinerator where the virus waited patiently. He wasn't sure what was going on upstairs, or how much longer the two agents could hold up against the assault, if they were alive at all. If the Wraith got here, that would surely mean they were dead. But if that was the case, where were the rest of the mercenaries? He had to find a way to complete his mission, which meant he had to find a way to defeat the Silver Wraith. To do that he had to be able to hurt it, or better yet, terminate it, and to achieve that goal he would have to find a way to get past it's armor, or get it to remove it. As the Wraith began slowly stalking him again, Xavier started to put together a plan in his head. It was incredibly risky, but if he didn't try something soon, he was a goner. The Wraith would simply continue to attack at it's insane pace, and sooner or later he would either make a mistake, or get too tired to match it. Either way spelled certain doom for him.

He slowly backed out into the taller, center portion of the room. If his plan was going to work, he was going to need space to maneuver. The Wraith followed him, seeming to once again be willing to toy with its prey. Perhaps the last exchange and his willingness to use unorthodox attacks had amused it. Whatever the case, it quickly dropped back into it's battle stance and twirled the blades, preparing to close in on its target. Xavier readied himself for the imminent onslaught, he had to time this just right. The Wraith stepped in, leading with a right slash that Xavier blocked, an overhead strike with the left sword which he also blocked, then the move he was waiting for, it spun and brought both swords down in a move that would no doubt rip Xavier in two. Xavier brought his sword up and blocked the strikes, parrying the blades off to the left with his sword, simultaneously, he pivoted his body so that he swung in with his back up against the Wraith's side. Suddenly, he let go of his sword with his left hand and quickly reached inside his jacket. In a split second, he removed the can of acid from his pocket and sprayed a stream over his own shoulder and straight into the mirrored faceplate of the Silver Wraith. Instantly it began to bubble and smoke, as the acid ate away at the material. The Wraith, suddenly blinded by the attack, began to swing wildly, unable to see through the corroding shield. Xavier easily dodged the wild swings and pivoted himself into position. Dodging another wild swing, Xavier executed a diagonal slash straight into the neck of the costume, figuring that this would be the most vulnerable point on the Wraith's armor. The strike landed a direct hit to the Wraith's neck, but to Xavier's horror, the sword once again bounced off the protective mesh. The Wraith blindly lashed out and caught Xavier in the face with an elbow and followed it up with a kick to his hip that sent him careening across the room and into a column with stunning force. Xavier saw bits of color in his field of vision from the impact and felt the ache in his hip, head, and at least a dozen other points from the assaults by the Wraith.

As he scrambled to his feet he spun toward the Wraith and was astonished by what he saw. The Wraith had laid one of its curved blades down on a counter and had pushed the hood back and unsnapped the headpiece of its armor. It then reached up and grasping the headpiece by the top of the mirrored faceplate, began lifting the entire helmet off. Long black hair spilled down out of the headpiece until finally it lifted it off completely, revealing a strikingly beautiful woman. Her long, black hair framed porcelain skin and severely high cheekbones. But most haunting of all were her eyes, gleaming electric blue orbs that stared at Xavier with an intensity he had never encountered. She looked mournfully down at the faceplate, now scarred to the point of being opaque, before glaring at Xavier. She threw it to the floor and reached up to rub her neck. The perfect skin already turning shades of blue and purple as the huge bruise, the only evidence of a blow that would have killed a normal person, formed. She continued rubbing her neck while staring at Xavier for several more seconds, before shaking her head.

"Tsk, tsk, tsk" she said, as she stopped rubbing her neck and shook her finger at Xavier. She then picked her sword back up and dropped back into her battle stance without another word. While desperately trying to shake the cobwebs from his head, Xavier peeled himself off the wall. Slowly he dropped back into a battle stance, hopeful in the thought that he had evened the odds somewhat, and that the Wraith was no longer invincible.

CHAPTER TWENTY-SIX

An Offer

Logan winced as another round of automatic weapon fire raked their makeshift shelter. The edges had been worn down but so far the middle of the tables were holding up, although twice he had jumped when the bullets had dented the part of the table directly behind his back. Martinez fired a couple of rounds in response and ducked back away before the hail of returning fire started. The barrage had definitely slowed in the last few minutes, no doubt they had started to figure out their strategy. Martinez had been the one to suggest firing back in a shorter burst, trying to draw their opponents into wasting needless ammo. As bullets ricocheted off the table Logan nudged his partner.

"You doing okay?" he asked over the hail of gunfire.

Martinez gave a sarcastic smile, "I've had better days..."

"I know what you mean," he replied. "How the hell did we get into this mess? Start of the day my biggest worry was figuring out what time to pick up Jenny tomorrow night."

Martinez grinned, "Jenny? So you're going out with that accountant again?"

"Well, I was," said Logan. "At this point I'm pretty sure it's off. I don't think she's into international bio-terrorist, at least it didn't say anything about that on her profile."

Martinez shrugged, "Oh well, at least you don't have to worry about picking a place for dinner. And without a job those steak houses she likes can get expensive."

Logan laughed, "Yeah it's crazy when you think about it. We've lost our jobs, everyone thinks we're some sort of terrorist, we're in a shoot out that we probably can't win and that's not even our biggest problem."

"That's pretty bad," replied Martinez, as she checked her clip. "What can be worse than that?"

"Oh, the fact that there's a pretty good chance that Xavier is dead by now and any minute that silver clad freak will bust out of the elevator door and finish the job it started on our teammates back at that warehouse." Logan shook his head. "I've gotta be honest, I'm starting to not like our chances at all. We're pinned down, outgunned, outmanned and we have absolutely no way out of it. We don't even have a keycard, so we can't even retreat to a lower level."

"True," replied Martinez. "I'm not digging it either and I can't say we've been in worse situations because quite frankly, we've never dealt with a situation even remotely like this. All we can do is hold the line. As far as the Wraith goes, if it comes back, I owe it. After what it did to George, I don't care if it is bullet proof, I plan on taking it out, even if that means taking myself with it."

Logan chuckled, "Man, have I told you how glad I am that you're on my side?"

Martinez was about to reply when Logan stopped her. "Hey have you noticed it just got really quiet again?"

The intermittent gunfire had ceased and once again all you could hear was the ventilation system as it struggled to keep up with the smoke from the gunfire. Logan put his hat on the end of a rifle and held it up so the top of it stuck out past the edge of the table, he expected a volley of gunfire but none came. Logan finally peeked out and saw nothing from the other side except small smoke trails, as if someone were smoking cigarettes.

Logan and Martinez shared confused looks. After a few more moments of silence passed, Logan broke the silence, "I really hope you guys have given up and are working out your terms for surrender."

"A cease fire has been declared," came a voice from behind the barricade on the other side of the room.

Logan glanced at Martinez, "A cease fire? Who declared it?"

"Here, take this," said the anonymous voice, as a hand slid a cell phone across the smooth floor.

Cautiously Martinez reached out and grabbed the phone. On the screen was a text message from an unknown number. It merely said "Hello".

"Do you agree to the cease fire?" said the voice across the room.

Logan looked at Martinez and then at the phone again, trying to piece together this latest development and shrugged. "Sure, why not?"

"What the hell do you make of this?" said Martinez as she stared at the phone.

"I don't know what to make of it," he replied, as he glanced over the table. "Well check this out!"

Martinez peeked out the space between the two tables that they had been using as a shelter. All six mercenaries, dressed head to toe in black special ops style gear, were standing up behind the cabinets, smoking cigarettes and talking amongst themselves. Logan and Martinez looked at each other, but before either could say anything, the phone made a beeping sound.

"It's another text, and you're not gonna believe this," said Martinez as she handed the phone to Logan. The text message said:

"Hello, I have declared a cease fire so that we can have a brief conference. We belong to a secret organization known as the Citadel. You are to be commended for staying alive and putting up an excellent fight. However the odds are not in your favor, as you probably realize. Our men are well armed and well trained. You cannot last forever and, sooner or later, you will be overrun. Given your considerable skills that would be a pity. Therefore, in order to expedite the situation and achieve our goal, the Citadel is prepared to offer you the sum of five million dollars each for you to join us, help eliminate Xavier Greene and retrieve the virus. This is a limited time offer so think it through. You have five minutes to reply. After that, the cease fire will end."

Logan sat staring at the phone for a moment. He glanced over the top of the table at the soldiers, still casually hanging out on the other side of the room. Logan held up his index finger and said "Give us a minute."

One of the soldiers nodded absentmindedly at him and went back to smoking his cigarette. Logan slowly dropped back behind the table.

"This whole situation is surreal," said Martinez as she re-read the text message.

"Tell me about it," Logan replied. "They're hanging out up there like a bunch of factory workers on smoke break and then we've got people we don't even know offering us more money than we've ever seen to help them. It's so strange."

"Yeah but I can tell you one thing," said Martinez.

"What's that?" said Logan, as he stared at the phone while trying to work a knot out of his aching shoulder.

"Five million dollars is a lot of money…"

CHAPTER TWENTY-SEVEN

The Battle Intensifies

Sparks and shards of glass rained on Xavier as he dodged the violent slash of the Wraith's twin swords. His belief that the Wraith would be more cautious once it had a weakness had proven false as, if anything, she had intensified her assault. Any sloppiness she had exhibited while invulnerable was now gone, and instead of moving forward with a reckless abandon, she had focused her attacks and seemed deadlier than ever. Due to this, Xavier had been on the defensive the entire time since the unmasking and hadn't been able to parry or counterattack at all.

Xavier ducked under one desk and leaped another, wondering how long he could keep up with the Wraith's relentless pace. The blades missed his head by inches as he side stepped another assault. He blocked two quick strikes and once again swung for the Wraith's head, but with that being her only weakness, she now put all of her effort into protecting it and easily deflected his assault. He was so caught up in blocking the Wraith's counter attack that he was caught off guard when his back bounced off of a wall. The momentary distraction almost proved to be a deadly mistake on his part, as the Wraith quickly tried to take advantage. She moved in and swung with one blade, which he deflected and followed up with a monstrous strike from the other blade. At the last second, reflexes that had been honed by years of training, allowed him to sidestep the blow, which missed his head by inches and lodged the blade deeply in the wall with a violent eruption of sheetrock. Sensing an opening, Xavier rolled his body weight against the Wraith's arm as she tried to pry the sword out of the wall and successfully caused it to fly out of her hand to the floor.

If losing the weapon bothered her, she didn't show it. Instead the Wraith continued to push her advantage. Pursuing Xavier out to the middle of the floor, it attacked with a massive downward slash aimed at carving Xavier in half. He blocked and parried the blow rolling their swords against each other, however, to his surprise, the Wraith flicked her wrist and Xavier's katana flew across the room, leaving him defenseless. Stunned at having been disarmed, Xavier backed slowly away as he swore he could almost see the beginnings of a cruel smile forming on the cold face of the Wraith. She stepped toward him and spun, bringing the full weight and speed of her sword down toward what she perceived as a helpless target. Instead of blocking or trying to run, Xavier stepped into the Wraith's attack and pivoted his body against hers, grabbed her wrist and used her own momentum to throw her across the floor, while simultaneously wrenching her sword from her hand. She tumbled across the tiles as he adjusted his grip on the crescent sword and moved forward, hoping to land a decisive blow. As he advanced however, the Wraith rolled through, leaped to her feet, and threw a roundhouse that connected with Xavier's arm, causing the sword to fly out of his hand.

Xavier backed away, stunned at how quickly she had once again disarmed him. He had taken pride in his mastery of the katana, and swordplay in general, but she had caused him to lose his weapon not once, but twice. In the meantime, the Wraith continued to stalk him as she had the entire time, completely self assured and unafraid, her cold blue eyes burning holes in his skull. She approached and threw several quick jabs that he blocked with ease, but those appeared to be a warm up, a test of his defenses. Xavier threw a strike of his own, only to have the Wraith glide toward him, past his fist and land a powerful knee to the midsection. He felt the air leave him and his body sag from the force of the blow, which she quickly followed up with a smashing strike to the face that sent Xavier reeling across the floor. He rolled and struggled to his feet as the Wraith peppered him with unrelenting body blows. Each blow felt like a sledge hammer strike delivered with an intense precision. Xavier felt his knees going weak and had to fight with everything he had just to stay conscious. The Wraith, sensing his weakness, grabbed him by the throat and shoulder and drove him backwards toward the nearest wall, intent on beating her victim to death. At the last second, Xavier regained his senses, shifted his weight, and using the Wraith's own momentum, drove her face first into the wall, while blasting her in the back of the head with a forearm strike. Blood flowed from the Wraith's nose, as it seemed stunned by the impact. Seizing on his momentary advantage, Xavier spun the Wraith around and swung her head toward a nearby computer console. However, at the last second she threw up her arms, braced herself on the console, and simultaneously wrapped her legs around Xavier's midsection. Before Xavier could react she pushed herself up and rolled forward toward the floor, smashing his face into the console. Xavier's vision blurred, as blood seeped into his sinuses from the impact with the plastic and glass computer. He stumbled backward, barely able to keep his balance as he bent over, almost collapsing to the floor. He opened his eyes and to his surprise the Wraith was still at his feet coiled up with her legs pulled against her chest. Like a striking snake, the legs shot upwards and connected with Xavier's chin. The immense impact sent Xavier through the air backwards, smashing his head on the tile in the process. The Wraith immediately rolled to her feet and searched feverishly for a weapon, while her opponent lay stunned on the floor.

Seconds felt like an eternity as Xavier struggled to fight through the crimson fog and back into consciousness. He opened his eyes just in time to see the Wraith gracefully spin and bring a sword down with deadly accuracy and force straight towards his head. At the last second Xavier managed to dodge and the sword struck the tile, smashing it into shards that ripped his face like miniature shrapnel. Running on pure instinct, Xavier quickly grabbed the Wraith's wrist before it could pull the sword free of the floor and wrapped his legs around her shoulders and throat, locking in a triangle choke, which simultaneously cuts off both an opponent's air flow, as well as the blood flow to their head. Without a moment's hesitation, the Wraith grabbed him with her free hand and started to shakily lift him off the ground. Frantically Xavier tightened the hold, squeezing with every ounce of strength. For the first time, he felt the knees of the Wraith buckle, as her strength appeared to fade and she slumped down to her knees, dropping him back to the floor. For the first time, there was an air of desperation in the Wraith's movements as she kicked wildly and pushed with her feet, feeling around for a weapon that she could use to free herself. Unfortunately, desperation and panic were not her ally, and her movements worked against her, as she accidentally kicked the sword that was left lodged in the tile. It clattered away across the floor, out of reach. With no weapon and her options fading quickly, the Wraith began punching frantically away at Xavier's side, but unfortunately for her, the blows had lost their sledge hammer like quality, and proved ineffective as her airway continued to constrict. Slowly, the Wraith's frantic attempts to escape subsided. Xavier held on, hoping beyond hope that she was fading into the abyss. Then, with some incredible reserve of strength, the Wraith began to rise back to her feet. Once she had gotten her feet in under her, she braced them and arched her back. Surely she didn't have the strength left to lift him? With supreme effort and inhuman focus, she started to rise and Xavier's blood ran cold as he felt his back leave the tile floor. She trembled under the effort, and had lifted Xavier almost two feet off the ground, when her strength gave out and she fell flat on her stomach on the floor, still trapped in the chokehold. Xavier cinched in the hold even tighter, and held it as he felt her go totally limp.

"That final gasp must have been the last of her strength," thought Xavier as he kept the hold locked fast around her neck. Normally he would have released the hold at this point and grabbed a weapon to finish her off, but this was no ordinary opponent. Until this point she had seemed almost unstoppable. He was taking no chances and continued holding on, intent on choking the very life from her.

Moments passed and he continued to hold her, sure that he had strangled the life from this almost mythical foe. Finally when she had laid motionless in the choke for what seemed like an eternity, he loosened the hold. Reaching down with one hand, he lifted up the head by it's silken black hair and looked at the pale face, it's complexion now a deep red from the lack of blood flow and oxygen. Suddenly, the eyes shot open and Xavier was frozen in horror by the intense, almost maniacal stare. One eye was blood shot, seemingly to the point of bursting, the other filled with blood from broken capillaries. To his terror, the almost blue lips parted and blood seeped from between her teeth and down her chin, as a guttural growl filled her throat. With inhuman speed and strength, she sprang to her feet and deadlifted Xavier into the air. It all happened so quickly he didn't have a counter. She had broken the choke and heaved him high into the air, no doubt intending on smashing the back of his head to a pulp on the floor below. However, neither of them had counted on the low hanging pipes in the ceiling, and as she lifted him with great force, Xavier's head struck the pipe, knocking him unconscious. His body went limp, and the shifting of his weight caused the Wraith to lose her balance and drop Xavier unceremoniously to the ground, his head bouncing with a dull thud. The combination of suddenly standing up after being in the choke hold for so long, combined with the blood rushing back into her head caused the Wraith to teeter, then lose her balance and fall backwards, her head soundly striking the edge of a countertop on the way down, before also smashing against the tile floor.

And so the battlefield went totally silent, the only sound the snapping of electrical wires in the devastated lab and the whirring of the air systems. Smashed tables, broken glass, and destroyed computer stations surrounded the two unconscious gladiators as they lay in pools of their own blood, complicit in their involuntary truce.

CHAPTER TWENTY-EIGHT

Message Sent

"So, you think I could get a small island for Five Million?" asked Martinez as she read the message once again.

Logan scratched his head, still trying to process the insane offer they had received from their mysterious would-be donor. His temples throbbed, no doubt due to the non stop stress they had been under, as well as the acrid smell of gun smoke that filled the air, making it barely breathable. His shoulders ached, his knees were shot from being crouched behind their makeshift barricade, and his ears rang from the nearly endless gunfire. Now not only was someone offering to end all this suffering, they were going to pay him and his partner an unimaginable sum of money.

"Earth to Logan, did you even hear me?" Logan looked up to see Martinez staring at him, her eyes bloodshot and tired.

"I figure you could, I think I saw something on TV about a couple buying an island for a cool 2mil, you would even have money left over," he muttered, rubbing his throbbing temples.

Martinez shook her head sarcastically, "See that's what I'm talking about. I would even have money left over."

Martinez smiled as Logan let out a chuckle. He pinched the bridge of his nose in a vain attempt to get the aching in his head to subside. "Whatever we're going to do, we're going to have to do it quickly, the clock is ticking."

"Yeah and what a choice it is, take the money and run, or continue to hold the line until we most likely get overrun or chopped up by that silver freak." Martinez sighed, "This is literally the worst situation we've ever been in."

"Worse than that time in Fresno?"

"Oh yeah, definitely worse than that, by a long shot. At least we had decent scenery there."

Just then they heard a loud tapping noise. After exchanging quick glances, Logan slowly raised his head to look over the barricade. The mercenaries still stood around on their side of the room, smoking cigarettes like factory workers on mid morning break. The one, who Logan assumed was the leader, pointed at his watch and then raised his eyebrows. Logan held up a finger, "Give me a little longer."

"What's up?" asked Martinez, as Logan lowered himself back to the floor.

"Looks like break time is almost over and our friends are getting anxious."

Martinez raised an eyebrow, "You know we could just take the money and walk away."

"Yeah true, but since when have we taken the easy way out? Besides, I don't like that guy rushing us. You know I like to take my time."

Martinez shook her head, "Oh I remember, that time in Phoenix with that pushy section chief…"

"Yeah, what was his name? Tyler? Can't remember his last name, just that he really got pissed about his car," replied Logan as he grinned in spite of himself.

Martinez shook her head, "Well as I recall you stole his keys from his desk and took his new Porsche in pursuit of a fugitive. You brought it back in less than new condition, and that's putting it nicely."

The agents laughed for a second, it felt good in the face of everything they were going through.

"You don't think we should take the offer do you?" asked Martinez as Logan sat contemplating his overturned stetson on the floor between them.

"Do you? I know it's easier and more likely that we live to see another day, but honestly I'm not sure I can live with selling out on Xavier. I know we barely know him, but think of what happens if we let them get their hands on that virus. "

Martinez shook her head, "I'm with you on that, but if these people are who they say they are then they could probably clear our records just like that." Logan shot his partner a glance. Martinez looked at him for a long time. "Yeah I know. I feel the same way, I just wanted to consider all options. If it wasn't for Xavier we wouldn't be in this mess, but if it wasn't for him we would also be dead."

Logan nodded "Yeah that's kind of where I'm at too. Xavier is the only reason we're not pushing up daisies or in federal custody. Besides, I'm starting to see his point. The virus needs to be destroyed, not only because of the damage it could do, but also the thought of some shadow organization holding the world ransom with it leaves a really bad taste in my mouth. So you cool with it?"

Martinez grinned, "You know I am. I've always backed any play you wanted to make, regardless of how insane it seemed at the time."

Logan sat back and placed his hat back on his head, "You remember that message we sent to that Bureau bigwig when he ordered us to stand down off that job outside of Albuquerque?"

Martinez looked at the phone and back at Logan, "You want me to text them that?"

"No, just type it, don't hit send yet. I'll let you know when." With that Logan adjusted his hat and stood up. The mercenaries all turned to face him, staring at the .357 that was hanging from Logan's index finger and thumb. With his other hand extended he slowly laid the large handgun on the edge of the barricade and held both arms out. The mercenaries flicked their cigarettes to the ground, not bothering to stamp out the butts, as the ground around them was littered with bullet casings. They all cautiously stared at the sight before them, like a cowboy from an old western, his hands outstretched in either direction like he expected the world's biggest hug.

Logan continued holding the pose while a grin slowly, almost imperceptibly formed on his face. The grin got bigger still, stretching his cheeks. The gunmen all glanced at each other nervously, not knowing what to make of the scene playing out in front of them. The grin continued to stretch way past what a sane person would consider normal. Just as it appeared his face would rip apart from the continually stretching grin, his lips finally parted, showing his gleaming white teeth. His mouth stretched open into a huge smile and finally in a loud voice he proclaimed "Comrades!"

He stood like that for several seconds and no one budged. The mercenaries looked at him and each other with confused looks on their faces. Logan stood with his stetson on, his arms outstretched, the smile on his face, looking for all intents and purposes like he had lost his mind. He looked back and forth at the group of confused armed gunmen, the smile plastered on his face, a few of the gunmen started to chuckle at the absurd display. Logan flapped his arms again and proclaimed "Comrades!", gesturing toward the group of mercenaries. The mercenaries looked at each other and Reese began to smile, relieved that this fool had taken the deal and come to his senses. This standoff had been going on way too long, and he was ready to finish the mission and get out of this godforsaken hell hole. He laughed and gestured back toward Logan "Comrade!" he replied as the rest of the men started laughing.

Logan also laughed, now they were all laughing openly, Logan making a huge show of taking off his hat and slapping his leg. The mercenaries all laughed at the outlandish display by the cowboy. Logan yelled "Comrades!" again as he placed his hat back on his head. The mercenaries all cheered and laughed at him, their guns, which had been wearily pointed at him, now hanging slack at their side as a few of them fished for cigarettes in their pockets.

Reese laughed at Logan and smiled at his men, happy that the mission was almost complete, laughing at the cowboy who was obviously feeling immense relief that he wasn't going to die by their hand, ready to take his payday and leave a rich man.

Logan continued to chuckle and gesture at the mercenaries before stretching his back in an over exaggerated stretch. He continued to smile and chuckle as he reached up with his left hand and adjusted his hat, seconds before his right hand swept up the .357 and leveled two shots in the blink of an eye, taking out two of the mercenaries. Logan dropped back behind the barricade a split second before the volley of bullets rained down on them. He glanced at Martinez, who just shook her head. Over the hail of bullets she asked "You just couldn't resist could you?"

Logan huddled lower, pushing himself further down and pulling his hat down tight to avoid the shrapnel from the assault. He leaned over close to Martinez, pulling her ear close so she could hear. "Now you can send it!"

Martinez hit send and tossed the phone over her shoulder, where it bounced across the tile floor. The last message sent showing on the screen:

KISS MY ASS

CHAPTER TWENTY-NINE

Back to Consciousness

The fog that enveloped Xavier seemed to stretch on forever, a thick haze that not only obscured his vision, but his thoughts as well. Xavier struggled, finding even his movement appeared to be restricted. He laid there for an undetermined amount of time, unable to find the will to move. It was then that he heard it, like the annoying buzz of an insect just out of reach, a faint scratching sound, barely perceptible to him. As it continued, the volume of it increased and it was as if the scratches were nagging at his thoughts, trying to tell him something. He slowly, with a supreme effort, rose to his feet and pushed forward through the haze toward the sound, determined to find the cause.

As he neared it, the fog seemed to thin, revealing the great dragon. It's horrible face twisted with anger and hatred, as it writhed inside of some sort of cage. Xavier stared at the great beast as it thrashed back and forth, pressing and testing the wooden cage. The dragon rolled over and over around itself, almost appearing to be liquid and each time it brushed against the cage, it strained and scratched, causing a sound not unlike nails on a chalkboard. Its pacing and testing of the cage continued until it noticed Xavier standing nearby. Suddenly the pacing stopped as its massive head pressed against the cage. The dragon's great eyes stared at Xavier as its head pressed on the bars, causing them to creak and groan, straining against its massive weight. It slashed the bars with its great claws, causing a much louder scratching sound, and Xavier felt himself want to shrink back away from it. However, the cage held and the great beast remained trapped. Feeling certain the beast could not escape, Xavier edged further forward, the haze thinning as he grew closer. It growled as it watched

Xavier draw near, scratching and clawing at the bars in frustration. He was close now, so close he could feel the warmth of the dragon's putrid breath. As he drew near he examined the bars, and to his horror, he saw that they weren't sticks or wood, but human bones. The entire cage appeared to be formed from various human bones, bound together somehow. Xavier took a step back, startled by the sight. The dragon roared and thrashed at the bars causing the scratching sound to become so loud that Xavier gripped his ears and shut his eyes, trying to will away the sound.

Now the haze was different, it was red and it filled his head like concrete, slowing his thoughts. He floated in this haze, slowly becoming aware of himself. Eventually he began to feel consciousness slipping in, peeling away the layers, pulling him to the surface. He could feel his body aching, his head feeling like it would split. If only he could make that infernal scratching sound go away. It still nagged at him, needling him, why wouldn't it just let him sleep? As consciousness continued to take hold he realized that he shouldn't still be hearing the scratching, why wouldn't it stop? Finally, he marshaled enough strength to open his eyes, only to quickly shut them as the fluorescent lights blinded him. His head felt like a dozen ice picks were entering his brain, his shoulder felt like it was partially dislocated, there was pain in at least a dozen points on his body. Then he heard the scratching again. Why wouldn't it just leave him alone? Finally he rolled over onto his side, rubbing and blinking his eyes until his vision slowly came back into focus. The sight he saw caused his blood to run cold. The scratching sound he continued to hear was none other than the Silver Wraith, dragging herself across the floor by her finger tips, blood pouring from an open wound on the back of her head and cascading down the bright silver outfit. With great effort, she was pulling herself along on her belly, clawing her way across the floor toward one of the crescent shaped swords, like some great silver snake looking for it's fangs.

Xavier felt the adrenaline kick in and began looking about for his own weapon, any weapon to defend himself with. He spotted his own sword lying on the tile floor, maybe eleven feet away. Frantically he began crawling for the sword, his shoulder aching with each pull as it felt like the cartilage would let go any minute. Suddenly he heard a clanging sound, like metal bouncing off tile and spun around, half expecting to see the Wraith hurtling toward him to deliver the death blow. Instead he watched in fascinated horror as the Wraith tucked the blade in her belt and continued crawling along, now heading for the second and final blade. Why had she continued on? Why didn't she come after him yet? Xavier stared mystified as the Wraith continued to struggle across the floor. Snapping out of his trance, Xavier realized he still needed to reach his own weapon and went back to the agonizing task of pulling himself across the floor. The pain in his shoulder was unbearable and he only allowed himself to look at his hands as he slowly pulled himself toward his goal.

Suddenly he heard the sound of the other sword, sliding off of the tile, his own weapon still a good two feet away. With as much of a burst of strength as he could manage, Xavier lunged forward and grabbed his sword, the pain shooting through his tortured body as he flipped over onto his back, struggling to bring the sword up, but determined to at least die fighting. But when he flipped onto his back and raised the sword, he found no incoming attack or sudden death, instead the Wraith merely continued to crawl toward the far wall. He watched as the Wraith slowly, painfully clawed her way to the wall, each pull a laborious effort that seemed to cause the flow of blood from the base of her skull to increase, the back of her silver outfit now covered with blood. The Wraith paused at the wall, as if absorbing the cold from the tile at its base. Seconds went by, and if it hadn't been for the occasional rise and fall of her breath, Xavier would have sworn she were dead. Then slowly the Wraith pulled herself up the wall and slumped into a seated position on the floor facing Xavier, her head hanging forward, her long black hair blocking her face. Xavier looked around him and found a desk nearby. He pulled himself slowly over to the desk and with much effort, pulled himself up into a seated position, slumping under the desk with his sword laying across his lap.

Breathing heavy from the effort he sat, looking across the room at the Wraith, which still hadn't moved. He felt his pulse pounding in his temples, the warm sensation of blood running down the side of his face, the ache of his shoulder as he tried to figure out if he had the strength to even stand up, much less fight. With any luck, perhaps the Wraith would pass out due to loss of blood, but he doubted he would get that lucky. Nothing about the Wraith had been normal so far and she had lived up to every bit of her mythical reputation.

At that moment, he thought he saw movement out of the corner of his eye and glanced over at his wounded opponent. The head of the Wraith lifted ever so slowly, the hair parting to reveal the pale skin, now stained with blood and bruises. Blood caked over her lip and chin, coughed up from enduring the choke hold for so long. Then her eyes met his, one eye completely filled with blood, a testament to the herculean effort it took to fight the triangle choke, the other eye badly bloodshot, the pupils burning a hole seemingly into Xavier's soul. For the longest time the two combatants just sat, facing one another, staring into each other's soul, measuring their worth. The Wraith studied Xavier's face for what seemed like an eternity, before finally opening her mouth and to Xavier's stunned silence, spoke.

"My name is Liliya Orloff."

CHAPTER THIRTY

Last Rites

Xavier's thoughts raced as he tried to process what he had just heard. That he knew of, the Wraith had never uttered so much as a word to anyone. The voice, raspy from the damage of enduring the choke hold for so long, had a heavy eastern European accent, but he couldn't quite place the country. He sat there lost in his thoughts until he glanced up and saw the Wraith still staring at him with those blood filled eyes, but now with one eyebrow slightly raised. He realized, to his astonishment, she was waiting on him to reply.

"I… I'm Xavier Greene."

She gave a slight nod at his reply.

"It is a pleasure to finally meet you Xavier Greene, after all these years I have finally found a worthy opponent. You are not like the others. Most men think their guns make them so powerful, only to be cut down like wheat before the scythe. They are all impotent and weak, their weapons useless against me, and I slaughter them like lambs." Xavier suppressed a shiver as the slightest hint of a smile crossed her lips. It passed briefly like a mirage and she continued.

"But you are different, your intellect is your weapon. You rely on your cunning and reflexes to get you through. I had heard rumors of you for sometime. Tales of one known as "the Silencer", who struck with a katana and never failed on a mission. I doubted such a person could exist, so when this mission came up, I accepted it. It was my chance to seek out this mysterious "Silencer" and test his skills versus mine, his blade versus my blade. I care little about this mission, or the virus, to me this power struggle is a bore and a waste."

Xavier raised an eyebrow, "Then would you object to allowing me to turn on the incinerator while we continue our chat?"

A glare from the Wraith shut him down, "When I was a child my father was a top intelligence official, loyal to a fault. But when the old guard came tumbling down and a new regime took power, we were hunted like dogs. My father had an old cabin in the mountains and we retreated there, thinking we had slipped away. Then the men came. I know their type well now, but then I was just a small child and the look of these men, hard and professional, terrified me. My mother hid me in the cupboard, and there I stayed. I heard them arguing, I heard the men assault my father and mother. I heard my mother's screams and then the terrible gunshots that cut them short.

My sobbing must have been too loud, because suddenly the men jerked open the cupboard door and snatched me out. I screamed and one man slapped me to the floor. The leader of these men grabbed me by the arm and jerked me up. He looked me over as I sniffled, afraid to dare move or make a sound. Finally he decided that I was too young to have fun with, and too small and scrawny to waste a bullet on. He told his men that he would leave me as a treat for the wolves and with that he threw me down into a pool of my parent's blood. I laid there terrified, alone in the cabin with no running water, no heat, and no power in the middle of the winter. I would have died there but for an old farmer who happened along and saw the door to the cabin ajar."

Once again Xavier thought he might see the slightest hint of a smile.

"He found me wrapped in a blanket, hiding in a cabinet. I was feral, emaciated, malnourished and in shock. My hair was matted down with my parents blood, my mind wild and desperate. He coaxed me out of my hiding place with some jerky he had in his pocket and eventually took me to his home. His wife had died the year before and he was all alone. So he raised me as his own, with no questions of what happened to my parents, or anything about the cabin. He kept me safe and warm, building my strength up with stew, and building my mind up by reading to me every night.

Eventually, I regained my health and he began teaching me to work, carrying firewood, and helping with the chores. He constantly worried about the coldness in me though, trying extra hard to break through my still icy exterior, but although I appreciated him for his hospitality, I refused to open up. One night he played the most beautiful fiddle music for me and it reminded me of my father during a happier time. I finally broke down and told him everything that had happened. After that I cried myself to sleep in his arms, and from then on, I was his daughter."

"He sounds like a wonderful man," said Xavier. Another stare by the Wraith froze him in his tracks.

"We lived together for years and I was content and happy with him. We would do chores, cook, laugh, and read stories all night. It was a wonderful time. I grew into a strong young girl, happy and content in my simple life. But then one day we went into town to the market and there was a robbery. It occurred just before we arrived. We came through the doors just as the robbers were making their escape. Papa didn't mean to detain the man, he was confused, he got tangled up with him. In the struggle the man thought he was trying to stop him, so he shot him. He died right there in my arms."

With a sigh, the Wraith sat and stared at the floor for what felt like an eternity, unmoving and barely breathing, as if going over that moment in her mind. Finally she brought her eyes back up to meet Xavier's and he could swear you could almost see a hint of moisture at the sides of them.

"That was the end of my good times. After that I was sent to the state run orphanage, a hellish place, full of leering adults and vicious children. I had never experienced such a place and that, combined with the loss of the person and life I loved, was almost too much to bear. Children picked on me and bullied me relentlessly, the price I paid for being an outsider. I never fought back, never said a word. I just took it, I didn't see the point in fighting back, I barely saw the point in living. One day I had just come in from recess and had finished showering. I was starting to get dressed, when two older boys slipped into the locker room. I screamed and ran, but they cornered me and started grabbing me. In that moment something snapped inside of me and I suddenly found that wild animal that I had been in the cabin so long ago. I screamed, but one of the boys shoved his arm in my mouth as they struggled to get me to the ground. I bit down hard and ripped a chunk of meat out of his arm, causing him to let go. As I continued to kick and struggle the remaining boy slipped on the wet tile floor and fell, smashing his head open. The blood poured from his head, filling the grooves in the tile and oozing toward the drain. I collapsed toward the corner as the other boy held his bleeding arm and stared at his friend lying in the growing pool of blood. He called me a bitch and told me I would pay for what I did, but he never finished the sentence. My blood was boiling as I grabbed a cricket bat that had been left propped up in the corner. Muscles that had been trained doing hard farm work brought the cricket bat down on the back of his head. It made a damp cracking sound as he skull split. He collapsed to the floor in a heap and I lashed out again, unable to control the rising and unfamiliar rage that filled my young body. When I had finished, I turned to the injured boy. He was crying and holding his head, the blood flowing across the tile. Could this possibly have been the predator that I was so scared of just moments ago? He and his friend had approached me like young lions on the prowl, I was prey, I was to be the conquest that helped them secure their manhood. Now he was nothing more than a mewling wretch on the floor. He finally realized I was standing over him and begged me to please not hurt him. Standing there, looking down at the pitiful creature, a righteous anger filled me. For the first time in my life I felt powerful. Without thinking, I lashed out with the cricket bat, over and over I smashed his head until everything became a crimson blur. Later teachers found me wandering around the recess field, still in my underwear, covered in blood. Then they found the scene I had left in the locker room."

For the third time, Xavier detected that ever so slight smile and his blood ran so cold he had to suppress a shiver.

"After that I was sent to a juvenile correction facility, an even harsher environment as you can imagine, but now that I had tasted the strength that my rage gave me, I no longer tolerated fools. I had several incidents during my time there. I eventually ended up in solitary, not for my protection, but for the protection of others. When I turned eighteen, they kicked me out onto the streets, not caring if I lived or died. It was a brutal existence, but I came out of the facility a much harder, stronger person than I went in. I decided to use my new found strength to avenge my papa and my birth parents.

I began targeting various gangsters and other unsavory types. I was sloppy and reckless, a blunt instrument filled with rage. However, I also had a growing talent, a singular focus to which I had dedicated my life. As luck would have it, my recklessness caught up with me and eventually, I was apprehended by the authorities. I had gotten too close to a mob boss who used his connections with the local police to get me off the streets. I was tortured repeatedly and left to rot in a cell, where I would await my execution. At that point it would have been sweet mercy compared to what I had been through. That would have been the end, had it not been for a government agent who heard of my exploits. They became convinced that I would be a valuable asset, a tool that could be honed into a powerful weapon. They came to me in my cell and offered me a job and a clean slate, and although I was reluctant, I didn't really have a choice. To live, no matter who I had to work for, was to have an opportunity to continue my personal vendetta. So I made a deal with the devil and gave myself over to their training. I was taught to take my rage and refine it, focus it. I became a finely tuned instrument of death, and rose through the ranks quicker than any recruit ever had. I was one of the elite assassins when regime change once again swept through the country. Unfortunately the loyalty that made me so valuable to the old regime, also made me dangerous to the new regime. I fled the capital, much like my parents had done during the last coup. In the end, I didn't fare much better than my parents. A squad of assassins caught up with me at a mountain chalet overlooking a river, hundreds of feet below. I fought well, but was badly injured in the ensuing struggle. Then they fired a rocket into the house and the explosion launched me through a bay window. I fell down the cliff and into the river, hundreds of feet below. I was presumed dead and to be honest, I would have been. My body was later found and recovered by agents from the Citadel, who had been sent to recruit me before I was killed in the coupe that they themselves started."

Xavier sat stunned trying to process this important piece of information. So the rogue faction of the Citadel had sent this task force to take them out after all. They had gotten terribly bold to make such an obvious power play, but after he had stolen the virus, it must have forced their hand. It now became all the more critical that he complete his mission.

"They took me to their labs and, while I was healing, they gave me experimental drugs that increased my endurance, speed and strength. Once I had healed from my multiple injuries, they trained me in a variety of martial arts, as well as fine tuned all of my skills to a level that I didn't believe I was capable of achieving. Then, they gave me the greatest gift of all, this silver suit which I wear now. The suit is made of graphene, which is thousands of times stronger than steel, but yet light as a feather. It was been woven and graphed onto this suit, making me for all intents and purposes, invulnerable."

Xavier was amazed at how similar the story of her recruitment was to his own, although he hadn't been given any experimental drugs. However he looked questioningly at the Wraith, "I've heard of graphene, but no one has developed the technology to manufacture it in a large enough quantity to use for your suit, not to mention how to even machine it into an outfit."

The Wraith merely raised a hand and gestured over her body, "And yet, here it is… Your comrades' guns and for that matter, your katana, have been totally ineffective against it. That should be all the proof you need." Xavier nodded to concede her point and she continued.

"So I have given you the gift of my story, Xavier Greene. A story that no one on this earth has ever heard, nor in all likelihood will ever hear again. I have given you this gift because you have given me the greatest battle of my life. You are indeed a worthy opponent and I respect you as a warrior, and a fellow student of the sword. Because of that respect, I want you to die an honorable death and, for a student of the sword, there is no more honorable death than to die by it. So I have given you this respite while I told my story. Now I will give you a little longer still. Rest up, marshal your strength, if you have any left, because the next time I rise, we will have one last duel and you… will… surely… die." With those words the Wraith put her head tenderly back against the wall and closed her eyes.

Xavier sat stunned as electrical wires snapped and popped in the background. He knew his body was wiped out, he had spent everything he had in the battle up to this point, his shoulder was probably dislocated or close, he was bleeding from multiple wounds, he probably had a concussion and he felt extremely weak and exhausted. He honestly felt like he would be lucky to be able to move, much less fight. As he sat under the desk he considered two options; he could scramble to his feet and attempt to make a break for the incinerator. She would probably kill him, but with the element of surprise he could probably pull the lever before she overtook him. On the other hand, he could lunge now and try to kill her. The problem with that tactic was she sat across the room from him and he was doubtful he could cover that distance before she realized it. A frontal assault at this point and from this distance would more than likely result in his death. He just didn't know what to do, for the first time in his career he felt totally defeated. She may not have killed him yet, but he was sure she had won. She hadn't just beaten him, she had gotten in his head so that now he was accepting his death as inevitable, merely because she said so. It was humiliating to feel so helpless and weak. Just as despair had started to drop it's veiled hood over him, a thought crossed his mind. An idea started to take shape. It was a long shot, but it was all he had left. Slowly, agonizingly, he pulled his fatigued and battered body into the Lotus position. Step by step, he began to strip each individual thought away from his clouded mind. Closing his eyes he continued to remove each and every vestige of his waking body, every ache, every pain, until all was quiet and he was left sitting in a dark room, on a wooden floor, with a single candle sitting before him. Watching the candle flicker, he slowly began working his hands through the nine symbolic cuts of the Kuji-Kiri.

CHAPTER THIRTY-ONE
A Final Reckoning

Liliya Orloff slowly allowed her eyes to open, the crimson fog that had clouded her mind easing as she did. The throbbing in the back of her head had continued, despite her best efforts to block it out. The bruise on her neck had been such an irritant to her, but was now the least of her concerns. She had underestimated Xavier Greene and paid a serious price for it. With great difficulty she swallowed and took a deep breath, immediately feeling the burning in her throat. She had come dangerously close to passing out when he locked in that choke hold, in fact, if he had held it a minute longer she might have been finished. But now she had rested and recovered a sufficient amount of strength to end this duel. It had been a risky gambit, giving not only herself but also her opponent time to rest, but she had no choice. Her body had been near collapse when she finally escaped the hold, and the damage done during the fall was even greater, as the intense pain and continued throbbing in the back of her head seemed to indicate.

She glanced over at her opponent, this strange man who was clearly outmatched by her, but had somehow nearly succeeded in doing what no other opponent had come close to doing. He was sitting in a pose that she recognized as either a meditative or spiritual pose of some sort and his hands kept moving through what appeared to be patterns of some sort. Perhaps it was a prayer ritual of some type? The thought of this annoyed Liliya, she had no time for such things and had never seen the practical purpose of them. Her entire life she had only counted on herself and had never seen the use in clinging to some higher power. Deep inside, anger flared up like a dormant volcano. She had given him time to rest and instead he spent it praying? What did he hope to achieve? Perhaps he hoped to make things right with his maker before she sent him to the afterworld? It didn't matter, in a few moments the whole thing would be over, then she could complete the mission and return home for some rest. Rest seemed like such a strange concept to her. Normally she didn't take a break between jobs but this time it would be necessary, she would have to heal from the damage that had been inflicted.

Slowly, painstakingly, she rose to her feet only to find she couldn't quite find her footing as vertigo threatened to send her back to the floor. Leaning against the wall she steadied herself, feeling the stiffness in her back and shoulders, the intense pain growing in the back of her head. After a few moments, it passed enough to let go of the wall and she stood, her arms feeling like lead. She slowed her breathing and concentrated, marshaling as much strength as her body would allow and spoke.

"Xavier." If he heard her, he gave no indication.

Annoyed and resisting the urge to cut him down where he sat, Liliya raised her voice, "Xavier!"

Xavier Greene's eyes opened with a graceful calm. Slowly he uncrossed his legs and rose to his feet, his eyes unblinking, yet serene, like a pond on a windless spring morning. Moving in an almost dreamlike state he bent down and retrieved his sword and assumed a stance that was both completely relaxed and yet completely prepared for an attack. His eyes remained calm and still, concentrating on the candle that he could still see in his mind.

Xavier's unnerving calm only seemed to enrage Liliya. Without saying a word, she stalked out to the middle of the room. This section of the room had a much higher ceiling and would allow for more freedom of movement, perfect for what she had planned. It was going to play out exactly how she envisioned it. Besides, Xavier seemed to work better when he had obstacles to throw in her way. This time she would give him nothing to work with. One on one he couldn't possibly match her.

In response to Liliya, Xavier walked calmly out into the middle of the room, his movements still carried a grace almost like a somnambulist, unnaturally smooth, as if he wasn't even aware of what he was doing. Liliya backed up against the wall on one side of the room and in response Xavier backed up against the opposite wall. Liliya raised both of her curved swords and assumed her battle stance, swinging her hips wide and crouching slightly to allow for her almost unnatural bursts of speed. Xavier assumed the Hidari Waki-no-Kamae, a samurai stance which translates to "down left". He slid his left foot back and held his sword along his waist on his left side, his eyes still showed complete calm and, although he was poised and ready, his body appeared completely relaxed.

Liliya stared at her opponent, at the sheer tranquility he exuded. It made her blood boil, her eyes, one filled with blood, showed raw, unmitigated rage, the same rage that had carried her through her entire life. This same rage that would carry her now as she unleashed it all on him. He would feel her fury, the same as everyone who had ever stood against her. No one had been able to stand up to it, and this would be no different. She would cut him down like everyone else and leave him lying a lifeless husk on the floor. Slowly a growl formed deep in her being that continued to build until she yelled a primal scream and charged forward.

In response, Xavier ran forward, still moving with an unnatural grace, his movements perfectly mimicking that of the samurai of ancient Japan. His feet moving gracefully, his sword by his side at the ready, his eyes a perfect stillness. The Wraith continued her charge and at the last second, she leaped upward into the air, spinning while drawing her swords to her sides to increase her momentum for the final blow. Xavier continued forward as she spun through the air toward him, his calm eyes following her every move. Suddenly, as she descended toward him, her arms sprang out, extending for the final strike. Xavier paused his advance and almost in a space between seconds switched his stance to Hidari-Hassou-no-Kamae, or "left up, even with chin" and leapt into the air toward his frenzied opponent. They struck simultaneously, three strikes cleaving through the air, three chances at death passing in a span of milliseconds. As they passed a sound, not unlike a knife cutting through wet meat, was heard and then the moment had passed and the two warriors landed, their momentum carrying them almost five feet apart, back to back.

The room was silent except for their labored breathing. In Xavier's mind the candle slowly faded and he returned to normal. A cold sweat slowly formed on his brow as he stood swaying and unsteady. Eventually, he became aware of the warm sensation of liquid spilling over his pants and down onto his shoes. Then slowly, but growing like wildfire, he felt the burning in his side, as one of the Wraith's blades had hit true and sliced a large gash. The pain grew stronger still as he began to grow weak. Suddenly, a loud noise startled him out of his stupor. It took a second to register, but it sounded like metallic clanging, like something falling to the floor.   Stiffly, and with great effort, he slowly pivoted around. The Wraith stood with her back to him, one sword lying on the floor, the other still in her hand. She swayed ever so slightly as blood began to seep from under her hair line, the bright crimson flow contrasting the blackened dried blood from her earlier wound. What began as a small trickle quickly became a cascade as her other sword fell to the ground with a loud clatter. Slowly the shape of her head began to distort, barely noticeable at first, but becoming more pronounced by the second, as the top of her head slowly started to slide off. Xavier stood, looking on in horror as the top of her skull slowly separated from the rest of her head, making a wet slurping sound as it did. Finally the top of her head, just above her eyebrows, slid completely off and fell to the floor with a horrific splat, like wet meat hitting a cold cutting table. For a few impossible seconds her body continued to stand, swaying as if showing one last act of defiance, before finally crumpling to the floor, her electric blue eyes staring straight ahead, one bloodshot, one full of blood, forever frozen in once last look of rage and confusion.

Xavier stood looking at the grisly scene as the blood began to pour out of her gaping head, forming a large pool that expanded over the tile. His eyes were following it when suddenly a wave of nausea overcame him and he collapsed sideways, grabbing a nearby desk to keep from falling to the floor. Shockwaves of pain swept through his body and he continued to hold on to the desk, clinging to it as unsteadily as he now clung to life. Sinking almost to his knees Xavier gasped for air, as black spots started to form before his eyes, his life force slipping out of him as surely as the blood that continued to seep out of his side. His face fell against the cool desk, it's surface bringing him a small modicum of relief, but only for a fleeting second. He felt his mind slipping into a haze, as if separating itself from the body before the final moments, when a vision appeared in his mind's eye. The dragon was there, still caged, but clawing and pressing in a frenzy, trying to escape it's imprisonment. To his horror the cage, though still holding, began to crack and give way.

With a burst of adrenaline and sheer willpower, Xavier rose back into consciousness. In a frenzy, he fumbled through the inner pocket of his jacket, the gash in his side sending spasms of pain through his very being, and pulled out a pouch. He tore at the tie that held the pouch tightly shut and as a convulsion of pain swept over him, spilled four pills out onto the counter. Again life started to slip away, despite his conviction and adrenaline. He clung to the counter, swept up in a blur of memories, trying desperately not to sink into the abyss. In his mind, he saw his teacher, Quan Li, back at the temple. He was explaining to him that the pills he had given him are made using an ancient technique by the apothecary of the temple and that just one pill can extend a man's life far past it's normal limitations. Slowly, inexorably, he pulled himself back from the brink again, and with his last reserves of strength he scooped up the pills and stuffed them into his mouth, forcing himself to swallow them. Then, with one last spasm, his body gave way, the last of it's reserves spent, as he slipped off the desk and fell to the floor.

Minutes passed as he continued to slip in and out of consciousness, completely unaware of his surroundings, his mind slipping through a continual, nonlinear series of memories and thoughts. The temple, his training, the dragon, the agents upstairs, it all drifted slowly past with no thoughts of failure or triumph, only a passing of random scenes. Then he felt it, he slowly started to become aware of something deep within him, almost like a spark, a slight warmth in the eternal cold. It continued to slowly expand, filling him with heat, like spring slowly thawing a winter field. It seemed to reach a tipping point, and then exploded, spreading like wildfire within him, warmth returning to his limbs, a sharpness starting to return to his brain. Like a swimmer fighting for the surface of the water, Xavier struggled to fight out of the memories which threatened to lull him into the grave. Fighting desperately, he struggled to reach the surface and, with a loud gasp, his eyes burst open, his lungs on fire, fighting for air. Born back into the world of chaos, despite his body's best efforts to embrace eternal sleep, Xavier Greene slowly returned to consciousness and the mission that still sat unfinished before him.

CHAPTER THIRTY-TWO

The Omega Option

Xavier stood clutching the counter, staring at the first aid kit in front of him. Although the pills had worked their magic, he felt as though he was holding on by a thread. As the throbbing, burning pain in his side reminded him, his energy was spilling out as quickly as his blood. If he lost too much, no amount of ancient medicine would be able to keep him alive.

He had managed to create a make-shift cane by locking his sword into it's scabbard, but the effort it took to actually stand up had nearly ended him. Now he held onto the counter, looking over the meager supplies in the first aid kit, and dreading what he was about to do. With great care, he slowly folded his jacket back out of the way and started unbuttoning his shirt. Ideally, he would have removed both his jacket and shirt, but in his current condition that just wasn't possible. Once the shirt and jacket were out of the way, he surveyed the damage. In his side was a deep gash, the blood pouring out of it. Xavier felt light headed just looking at it and had to look away to steady himself. He knew he needed medical attention, but he had no idea if that was even possible, or if he would even make it back to the surface. He glanced over his shoulder at the remains of the Silver Wraith, her electric blue eyes still staring at the ceiling.

"This may yet end up a draw," he said as he eyed his former opponent.

His gaze lingered on the Wraith for a few more moments, but a sharp pain in his side brought him back to task. He uncapped a bottle of antiseptic and, after steadying himself with a few deep breaths, poured it into the open wound. Immediately searing pain overtook him like a thousand hot pokers driving into his side and he screamed, the bottle bouncing off the floor and rolling away. The intensity of the agony continued to increase as he clung desperately to the counter, trying his best to ride it out. After what seemed like an eternity of torture, it ebbed, and he felt like he could breath again. His body relaxed slightly and he straightened up, leaning against the cabinet to fight the persistent lightheadedness that threatened to take him to the floor once more. His bloody fingers probed the first aid kit looking for, and finally grasping, a tube of antibiotic ointment. With trembling hands, he filled the gash with the ointment and immediately felt a renewed burning sensation. He was relieved to find it didn't hurt nearly as bad as before. He assumed the antiseptic must have burnt what was left of his nerve endings, and for that, he was lucky. Carefully he worked to tape it shut, wiping away blood so the tape would actually stick. Finally, he applied two large pads on top of each other, taped them in place, and wrapped more tape around his body to keep the pressure on it. Satisfied that he had done an adequate job to prolong his life a little longer, Xavier buttoned up his shirt and using his sword as a cane, hobbled his way over to the incinerator.

He looked over the controls and made sure everything was still as he had set it, the Wraith's dagger still stuck in the panel. Once satisfied that the settings were intact, he reached over, primed the burner, and when it was ready, he reached for the ignition lever. Just as he was about to pull it, he caught a glimpse of the virus sitting in the cylinder within the incinerator. Perhaps it was the meds, or perhaps it was shock, but Xavier could almost see the dragon rolling around in the viscous liquid of the virus. This little vial had caused so much death and destruction and contained the potential to cause so much more. After one last glance, Xavier pulled the lever, and nothing happened.

Xavier pulled the lever again, nothing. Again he pulled the lever, nothing. In a fit of exasperation he slammed the lever down again and again. But the incinerator sat there, silent and unwilling.

"Goddamnit!" Xavier exclaimed, as his hand slammed into the control panel.

"HOW MAY I BE OF ASSISTANCE?"

The voice startled Xavier, and he whirled around with his back to the incinerator. The room lay empty before him, all sparking wires and overturned furniture from his titanic struggle with the Wraith.

"How may you be of assistance?" he asked aloud, a slight feeling of foolishness creeping into him, as he realized he was responding to a voice that may have been a figment of his imagination.

"YOU PRESSED THE HELP BUTTON, I AM HERE TO ASSIST YOU."

Xavier turned to the incinerator and noticed the button labeled "Voice Activated Automated Help" where he had smashed his fist into the incinerator in frustration. He turned back around and noticed that on the work station closest to him was a computer that was still intact. It took him a moment, but he finally realized that the message on the screen matched the voice that had startled him. Finally he spoke, "The incinerator is not working, can you help?"

"THE INCINERATOR IS OFFLINE, IT HAS BEEN DAMAGED."

Xavier glanced at the Wraith's dagger, still plunged into the incinerator panel, and shook his head.

"QUITE A FEW SYSTEMS ARE DAMAGED IN THIS ROOM. WOULD YOU LIKE A LIST OF THEM?"

"That won't be necessary. Can we get the incinerator back online? There is a virus in it that must be destroyed."

"I'M AFRAID THAT IS NOT POSSIBLE. IT WILL REQUIRE REPAIR BEFORE IT CAN BE OPERATIONAL AGAIN."

Xavier shook his head at his turn of bad luck. It had been almost impossible for him to get to this lab and set up the destruction of the virus. Now they had been pinned down here for far too long. There was no telling how many factions had zeroed in on the location and were waiting to ambush them outside. This had to somehow end here.

"Computer, I have an extinction level virus in the incinerator, it is essential that it be destroyed now. What options do we have? Is there another incinerator on the premises?"

"NEGATIVE, THERE IS NO OTHER INCINERATOR. THE ONLY OPTION LEFT IS THE OMEGA OPTION, WHICH IS A COMPLETE SELF DESTRUCTION OF THE ENTIRE FACILITY. IT WAS CREATED

AS A FAIL SAFE IF THERE WAS A MISHAP AT THE LAB IN ORDER TO PREVENT A VIRUS FROM ESCAPING."

Xavier leaned against the incinerator, pressing his forehead against the cool, metallic surface. He thought about the agents who were above risking their lives to help him complete the mission. He thought of everything he had been through and how it had come down to this. Sighing in resignation, he knew what he had to do. He glanced at the remains of the Wraith, "I guess it's going to end up as a draw," he said to his lifeless opponent.

"Computer, I would like to activate the Omega Option."

"PLEASE SCAN YOUR KEYCARD TO CONFIRM"

Xavier fumbled in his jacket, found the keycard and swiped it at the computer terminal.

"AUTHORIZATION CONFIRMED. WOULD YOU LIKE TO LOCK DOWN THIS LAB OR THE ENTIRE COMPOUND?"

Xavier again thought of the agents, "This level only. Leave the upper levels open." He figured there was no use in trapping the agents in, if they were still alive.

"ONCE ACTIVATED, HOW LONG TILL SELF DESTRUCT?"

"Fifteen minutes."

"PLEASE NOTE THE MAIN ELEVATOR ON THIS FLOOR IS INOPERABLE DUE TO DAMAGE SUSTAINED ON AN UPPER LEVEL. WOULD YOU LIKE TO USE AN ALTERNATE ESCAPE ROUTE?"

He was puzzled by this, "Computer, I thought you said this level would be locked down?"

"IT WILL BE. BUT THERE IS A TWO MINUTE DELAY TO EVACUATE ESSENTIAL STAFF, IF FEASIBLE, BEFORE THE LOCK DOWN COMMENCES."

* * *

"So even with the elevator out of commission, there is still a way out of the lab?"

"YES. THAT IS CORRECT. WOULD YOU LIKE FOR ME TO FORWARD YOUR KEYCARD INFORMATION INTO THE VARIOUS ENTRY POINTS TO EXPEDITE YOUR EXIT?"

"Computer, show me a map of the alternate escape route."

A map popped up on the computer screen, showing the route. Xavier scanned the screen, and for the first time in a long while, a smile slowly formed on his face...

CHAPTER THIRTY-THREE

Time to Leave

The alarm rang out, it's pulsing blare overpowering even the endless sound of gunfire in the upper labs.

WARNING. OMEGA OPTION ENABLED. THIS FACILITY WILL SELF DESTRUCT IN FIFTEEN MINUTES.

The gunfire ceased and the room was silent except for the pulse of the alarm. Logan and Martinez looked at each other in disbelief as if trying to process what was happening.

"No way," said Martinez as she stared at Logan. "You think Xavier actually pulled it off?"

"I have no idea," replied Logan as he felt his headache growing with every pulse. "Last I heard, blowing up the entire lab wasn't the game plan."

Martinez nodded, "Well maybe you're not the only one who knows how to improvise."

WARNING. OMEGA OPTION ENABLED. THIS FACILITY WILL SELF DESTRUCT IN FOURTEEN MINUTES.

Logan cupped his hands and yelled over their makeshift barricade, "Hey! Are you guys hearing that? It's a lost cause, your friend blew it. There's no point in continuing this fight because we're all going to get blown to hell. I say we call a cease fire and get out of here."

On the other side of the room, Reese closed his eyes trying to wrap his head around the situation. This was bad, really bad. Apparently the

Wraith had failed, and now their mission appeared to be a wash. They had no way of knowing what was going on below, the Wraith had taken the only keycard. As if that wasn't enough, according to the voice over the intercom, they only had fourteen minutes until the entire place would self-destruct.

Malachi shifted around to face him, "What's the call boss? You think that silver freak couldn't get the job done?"

Reese chewed his upper lip, "I have no idea, for all I know the Wraith grabbed the package and is leaving us for cannon fodder."

"Well we need to make a choice soon or it'll get made for us," replied Malachi, "My opinion, we need to haul ass."

Seconds later, Reese yelled across the room, "Okay, we're going to pull out, don't shoot us in the back and we won't shoot you when you reach the top. You go your way, we go ours, agreed?"

"Sounds like a plan!" Logan shouted back.

Abruptly the remaining mercenaries jumped up from behind their barrier and ran up the stairs towards the lobby. Logan watched cautiously from behind what was left of the table as they retreated and a few seconds later, he and Martinez pulled themselves to their feet, knees aching and popping from huddling on the hard, tile floor and started toward the stairs themselves.

"Are we really just going to go running up the steps and out of this place?" asked Martinez as they made their way toward the staircase.

"What choice do we have? It's that or stay here and get blown to bits." Logan replied.

They were almost at the stair well when they heard a voice from the top of the stairs, "Goodbye 'comrades'!" Then they heard it, a rhythmic pinging as something metallic bounced down the stairs. Logan saw it as it cleared the stairwell. A grenade bounced out onto the tile floor. In a split second he turned and shoved Martinez over the nearby rubble of a desk. Then everything went up in a flash of light and fury.

Martinez laid prone behind the desk in the rubble, the ringing in her ears giving her surroundings a surreal, dreamlike quality. Her mind reeled as she tried to remember where she was and what had happened. She remembered running toward the stairs and there was a sound, then Logan had shoved her backwards and something... There was a flash of light and concussion wave that had hit her in the chest, knocking the wind out of her. Still groggy and with an aching in her head, Martinez struggled to her feet and stumbled through the remains of the office, barely able to breath in the smoke. Shattered desks and cabinets littered the room, most of which was in flames. In front of her the entryway, where moments ago a staircase existed, was a hopeless pile of debris and shattered concrete. There would be no exit that way. The thought rattled around in her head, they were trapped in this burning room with the whole facility about to go up around them. The shock of the thought finally snapped Martinez back to her senses. Where was Logan?

"Logan! Logan!" she cried, As she shuffled through the twisted, gnarled debris. After a few moments, she found him behind the barricade where the mercenaries had been hiding earlier. Logan was covered in fragments of concrete and other shrapnel, nicks and cuts adorned his face, and his shirt was shredded, but his leg was what caught Martinez's attention. A large gash had been torn just above the knee and blood was gushing out onto the tile floor. Without thinking, she immediately whipped off her belt and wrapped it around his upper leg. As she pulled it tight Logan groaned in pain.

"Rise and shine," said Martinez as she struggled to fasten the belt around Logan's leg.

"What happened?" Logan groaned, "Where's my hat?"

Martinez chuckled despite herself, "Seriously, you're worried about that? You want the bad news or the worse news?"

Just then the garbled voice came over the broken speaker,

"WARNING. OMEGA OPTION ENABLED. THIS FACILITY WILL SELF DESTRUCT IN TWELVE MINUTES."

"Well it beat me to it," said Martinez as she held the belt tight.

"What's the other bad news?" asked Logan as he struggled to remain conscious.

"The other bad news is that you may bleed to death before we get incinerated,"

Just then, they heard a scraping sound and a panel in the wall slid open, pushing against the debris that littered the floor. Xavier Greene slowly hobbled out of the opening. Martinez was shocked by his appearance. Tattered and ragged, Xavier looked like he had literally been to hell and back. His face was littered with cuts, his suit and pants had bloody slashes where he had obviously been cut. He leaned on his sheathed sword like a cane and to her, it appeared that was all that was keeping him on his feet. As he drew closer she saw his left side and gasped aloud. The entire left side of his shirt and pants were caked in dried blood. She wondered how he was still alive after so much blood loss. Then she looked up at his face and to her surprise, he still seemed extremely alert, his eyes darting around the room.

"Boy, you guys know how to party..." Xavier quipped to no one in particular, as he surveyed the damage to the room. Then his eyes came to rest on Logan and a grave look came over his face. With great effort and a grunt of pain, Xavier lowered himself to the floor beside Logan and looked at the mangled leg. He took the belt from Martinez and tugged at it, attempting to tighten it around the injured leg.

"Agent Martinez, see if you can find the first aid kit, it should be somewhere on that side of the room, near that medic symbol on the wall," he nodded in the direction of the far wall and Martinez jumped up without saying a word. She scrambled through the pile of wreckage, all the while wondering how Xavier was even standing, much less alert at this point. Finally she found the case with the medic alert symbol under a pile of wood and granite.

"Got it!", she exclaimed as she scrambled back to Logan's side.

"Hold him down," commanded Xavier as he ripped open the case. Quickly he surveyed the contents of the well stocked case and grabbed a few clips, normally used to fasten gauze.

After bending them slightly, Xavier glanced at Logan, "Sorry about this..." and he thrust his hand into the open wound. Logan screamed in pain and thrashed about as Martinez tried her best to hold him down. Working quickly, Xavier located the severed artery and using the improvised clips from the kit, clamped it shut as best he could.

"What the serious fuck?" exclaimed Logan as Xavier reached into the kit and pulled out the antiseptic.

"I'm sorry," said Xavier as he laid his hand on Logan's arm, "it only gets worse." He then dumped the antiseptic into the wound and Logan howled with pain before passing out. Xavier then grabbed a tube of antibiotics and emptied the entire thing into the wound, as he had done to himself earlier.

"Quick, help me rip open these cotton pads," he said to Martinez as they both scrambled to open all the cotton pads contained in the kit. As each one was opened, Xavier quickly stuffed it into the gaping hole in Logan's leg. When they were finished stuffing the pads in the wound he wrapped it with gauze and taped it shut with as much pressure as he dared to put on it.

"WARNING. OMEGA OPTION ENABLED. THIS FACILITY WILL SELF DESTRUCT IN SEVEN MINUTES."

With that Xavier turned to Martinez, "Okay Agent, it's time to go!"

"Good luck with that!" replied Martinez, gesturing toward the ruined remains of the stairwell.

"Fortunately, we aren't going that way. Help me get Logan to his feet and I'll show you," said Xavier as he moved to lift Logan's shoulder and neck. Martinez moved around to the other side and grabbed Logan's other shoulder and together they worked to drag him to his feet. The effort seemed to cause Xavier a great deal of pain and he swayed slightly back and forth.

"Easy," said Martinez, "I can't carry you both."

Xavier closed his eyes and steadied himself. Then he nodded toward the far wall and they made their way across the room, Agent Logan propped up between them. As they reached the wall, Xavier reached out and flipped open a keypad that had been hidden by a square panel. He punched in a code and the wall opened to reveal an elevator. Martinez marveled at this hidden escape route and for the first time she started feeling a little hope that they would make it out after all.

"WARNING. OMEGA OPTION ENABLED. THIS FACILITY WILL SELF DESTRUCT IN SIX MINUTES."

Xavier pressed the button for the highest level and the doors closed. For a second all was mercifully quiet. Martinez leaned her head back and breathed in the clean air, it was the first time in what felt like an eternity that the air didn't smell like ordinance or smoke.

"What happened to the virus?" she asked, even though she felt like she knew the answer.

Xavier stared straight ahead for a moment and sighed, "The incinerator was damaged so the Omega Option was the only way to make sure."

Martinez nodded, "What about the Silver Wraith?"

Xavier caught her gaze and slowly shook his head then directed her gaze to his side, still caked with blood and gore, "A souvenir…"

Martinez thought about asking how he was still alive, but she felt the elevator slow and the moment passed. There would be time for that later, if they survived.

CHAPTER THIRTY-FOUR

Just in the Nick of Time

The trio stepped off the elevator into the stale warm air. In front of them was a long tunnel, in the distance they could see dim lights. They shuffled toward the light, dragging a barely conscious Agent Logan between them, until it ended at another tunnel with a small car mounted on rails, not unlike a roller coaster. Martinez and Xavier looked at the car and then glanced at one another.

"At least we don't have to walk anymore," said Martinez as they lowered Agent Logan into the backseat of the car.

"WARNING. OMEGA OPTION ENABLED. THIS FACILITY WILL SELF DESTRUCT IN FOUR MINUTES."

Xavier gingerly lowered himself into the seat beside Martinez as she hit the ignition and pushed the throttle forward.

"Here we go, hang on!" said Martinez, as Xavier was thrown back in his seat by the acceleration.

The walls of the tunnel whirled past in a blur as the car raced down the tracks. As they continued down the tunnel, daylight became visible in the distance. The light grew as they continued forward until they suddenly realized the tracks ended in a large padded barricade.

"Oh shit!" exclaimed Martinez as she let off the throttle and fumbled for the brake lever.

The car quickly decelerated slamming Logan's head against the back of the seat and forcing both Martinez and Xavier against the dashboard.

"We're not going to stop in time-" Xavier was cut short by the impact of the car striking the barricade.

Despite the last minute deceleration the car still hit the barricade with enough force to throw Xavier out the side of the car and smack Logan into the back of their seat and into the floor.

"Ow, what the fuck?" groaned Logan, as Xavier struggled back to his feet beside the car.

Martinez, who had managed to stay in the car by hanging onto the brake lever, slid out of the car and walked around to where Logan lay prone in the back floorboard.

"Hey, any landing you can walk away from..." she cracked as she reached down and started helping Logan up. Xavier helped her support Logan once again and the three of them walked out of the tunnel into the open desert air.

"WARNING. OMEGA OPTION ENABLED. THIS FACILITY WILL SELF DESTRUCT IN TWO MINUTES."

Xavier looked around at the vast expanse that surrounded them. They were on the end of the ridge, far above the lab below. Around them the arid landscape stretched on to the horizon, the oppressive sun beaming down upon them. "We should be far enough away up here," said Xavier as they lowered Logan to the ground underneath the shade of a rock outcropping.

Just then, gunshots rang out and both Xavier and Martinez instinctively ducked. They could hear the shots continuing in the valley below as another volley rang out in reply. They left Logan in the shade and slowly made their way to the edge of the cliff.

From their vantage point they could see a cluster of black SUVs gathered in front of the lab's entrance. A group of men in combat gear were using the trucks for cover as they fired on Reese and Malachi, who were huddled in the entrance of the lab.

"We don't have the virus, it's gone! For God's sake, let us out. This place is going to blow!" screamed Reese as the men in the trucks raked the front of the lab with another round of gunfire.

"WARNING. OMEGA OPTION ENABLED. THIS FACILITY WILL SELF DESTRUCT IN ONE MINUTE."

Reese and Malachi hid behind columns at the front of the lab, desperately trying to think of a way out. Outgunned and trapped, they did the only thing they could and continued to pop out from behind the columns long enough to return fire before having to take cover from the onslaught of the heavily armed men. They were pinned down tight with no way out and they knew it. Reese was trying to assess their options, trying to come up with something to say that might save their lives, when suddenly the loud speaker blared again.

"WARNING. OMEGA OPTION ENABLED. CLEAR THE GROUNDS. THIS IS YOUR LAST WARNING. TEN, NINE, EIGHT, SEVEN…"

A low rumble started to reverberate from underneath their feet. Desperation kicked in and they both jumped to their feet and ran out the front of the lab into the hail of gunfire. Reese immediately took two rounds to the chest and Malachi flinched waiting for another round of gunfire to find him, only it never came. He opened his eyes, and to his shock, saw the men jumping into the SUVs, while others scattered across the parking lot. However, the scene seemed strange to Malachi, like everything was shimmering and distorting slightly. At the same time, he realized that his feet were burning in his boots, like hot coals being stuck to his soles. Malachi started to hop, while alternating feet. As he did he realized that the shimmering was due to heat waves radiating off the ground. If he stood still, his goose was, literally, cooked.

In a last ditch effort he sprang into a full run, trying desperately to get away. He spotted a nearby SUV and sprinted for it, hoping the keys were still in it. But as he ran, his boots began to stick to the asphalt, leaving strings of rubber behind him. He was about ten feet from the truck when the asphalt itself began to take on a soft quality, like running in soggy, loose tar. As he struggled to run his lungs felt like they were going to explode from the overwhelming heat. His skin and eyes burned from the increasing temperatures, his skin starting to crack as he was roasted alive.

Finally it was too much for him to take. He stopped running, no longer caring about the burning in his feet, his shoes smoldering as the fabric began to burn. The tires on the SUV exploded as it sagged into the now molten asphalt. In the extreme heat, Malachi couldn't breath, his lungs scorched from the superheated air. Finally, he passed out and fell face first into the sludge with a sizzle.

Xavier and Martinez looked on as Malachi burst into flames. The other mercenaries were scattered across the parking lot in similar flaming heaps. The SUV's gas tanks started randomly exploding, one by one sending up huge fireballs into the air. As the inferno continued to intensify, the light poles and fencing started to warp and sag, the palm trees that lined the parking lot burst into flames and even the building appeared to start to melt and collapse from the unbelievable heat.

With a loud groaning noise, like the moan of a dying beast, the ground itself collapsed in, taking the remains of the soldiers, the SUVs, the parking lot, and the facility all with it into a huge flaming pool of liquid metal and flames. Xavier and Martinez stared into this flaming abyss, rolling and churning like the mouth of hell itself. The heat was so intense that after a few seconds of being mesmerized by this gaping inferno, they were forced to drop back behind the ridge. There they sat gasping for a few minutes, trying to absorb the horror of what they had just seen.

CHAPTER THIRTY-FIVE

Struggle to Survive

After one last glance over the ledge at the burning hellscape, they made their way back over to Agent Logan, who was still lying where they had left him, and to their surprise, he was stirring ever so slightly. Martinez crouched beside him and rubbed his forehead. He opened his eyes slightly and moaned.

"What did I miss?" he asked weakly.

"Oh, just the after game fireworks," replied Martinez as she cupped his head in her hands.

"Man I always miss the good stuff..." mumbled Logan as he once again lapsed into unconsciousness.

Just as she was about to ask Xavier what their next step was, Martinez heard a wet, raspy cough come from behind her. Xavier had slumped down against the rocks, blood from his cough splattered against it's surface. Weakly, he fumbled through his jacket pocket and pulled out a set of keys that he tossed to Martinez.

"There is a medical kit in the back of the car. Logan and I need it if we're going to make it long enough to receive medical attention," he said in a weak voice. Totally spent, he sagged back against the rocks. "Hurry..."

Martinez glanced back at Logan and without a word, sprinted over the ridge. All was quiet for a long time, with just the sound of Xavier's labored, wheezing breaths.

Blinking his eyes, Logan slowly became aware again. "Xavier?"

"Yes Agent Logan?" Xavier replied weakly.

"Is this a normal day at the office for you?"

"Well," replied Xavier, "more or less."

Logan coughed a short cough and cleared his throat, "Then I really hope you can help Martinez and I get our jobs back, because your job sucks."

Xavier stared at Logan for a few seconds before they both broke into a grin and, by some miracle, he found himself laughing. It was short lived however, as the laughing quickly devolved into a coughing fit, followed by a wave of pain that caused Xavier to pass out once again.

Xavier felt himself nudged slightly out of his slumber by a slight bump to the bottom of his foot. He quickly forgot about it and continued to drift in his stupor, until a sharp blow to the sole of his shoe pushed him all the way back into the world of the living. Groggily, he opened his eyes and, after blinking a few times to sharpen his focus, saw a man with a long beard in black paramilitary gear, standing over him, an automatic rifle resting on his arm.

"Where is Tears of the Dragon?" said the man as he stared down at Xavier.

Xavier stared back, his eyes indifferent to the current situation and instead of answering, he merely nodded toward the cliff, where the smoke could still be seen swirling from the still smoldering wreckage.

The man rubbed his beard for a moment before shaking his head in anger "Goddamn you. All of that hard work for nothing."

Xavier continued to calmly observe the man, "And all of those innocent people spared."

The man grimaced as he shook his head, "All of those people living in oppression and poverty, while the one's who pull the strings live in unimaginable luxury. This was supposed to be the end, no, the new beginning. The odds would have been evened, a new society could have been born."

He picked up Xavier's sword and considered it for a moment.

"What is done is done. At least we won't have to worry about you any longer."

He stepped forward as he attempted to draw the sword, but it wouldn't budge, Xavier had locked it shut so he could use it as a cane. The man shook the sword with frustration, struggling to open it. Finally, he twisted it just right and the sword released from the scabbard. He withdrew the blade and threw down the scabbard, staring at Xavier as he raised it over his head. Just as he was about to bring the sword down for the killing blow, a shot rang out. For a second, he hung there, frozen in the air like a marionette with the strings cut. Blood slowly seeped down his forehead as he slumped to the ground, landing beside Xavier in the dirt.

Agent Martinez stood at the edge of the clearing, pistol in hand and a medic kit draped over her shoulder.

"A sight for incredibly sore eyes," said Xavier as she approached them.

"Looks like I got here just in time, are you okay?" she asked as she grabbed the man by the foot and pulled him over out of the way.

"Only temporarily I'm afraid," replied Xavier weakly. "Look through the kit, there should be a pouch of pills in it."

She rummaged through the knapsack that served as the medical kit, "Found them!" She opened the small canvas bag and found eight pills.

"Excellent," replied Xavier. "Please give me two pills and only one to Agent Logan."

Martinez handed Xavier the pills and a bottle of water that she retrieved from the kit. She then tilted up Logan's head and got him to drink some water and take the pill. Xavier laid still for a few minutes before he took a deep breath, stood up, and approached Agent Logan.

"How in the hell?" she asked, as Xavier rummaged through the medical kit. "A few minutes ago you seemed to be at death's door and now you're up and moving around?"

"No time to explain," said Xavier as he pulled a bottle of liquid and a small container of herbs from the knapsack. He placed a bowl he had retrieved from the kit on the ground and mixed together the liquid and herbs in it to form a paste. He then, as gently as he could, removed Logan's bandage from his leg and pulled the gauze out of the wound.

"I didn't want you to give all the pills to Logan yet, because this would be a lot worse if he was awake." Xavier explained as he packed half of the paste into the wound. He then rewrapped the wound with a clean bandage from the medical pack.

"Now for the real fun part," he said, as he pulled his jacket and shirt back and removed his own bandage.

Martinez gasped at the severity of the wound, not knowing how he was even still alive, much less functioning. The gaping wound was covered in dried blood and turning bright red as infection was starting to set in.

"It's going to be up to you to finish applying the bandage," said Xavier as he prepared the paste, "I'm pretty sure I'll pass out from the pain of what I'm about to do." Without waiting for her reply, Xavier wadded up the paste and stuffed it into the wound. He screamed in agony as he stuffed more paste into the gash, pain spreading from the wound throughout his body, threatening to push him out of consciousness. At last he succumbed to the pain and slumped back against the wall.

Martinez worked quickly and finished dressing the grisly wound. Once it was wrapped up tight she gently shook Xavier until he woke up.

"Thank you for that, I certainly owe you a lot today."

Martinez shook her head, "No worries, now how are we going to get out of here? I can't carry both of you, but I figured we need to leave before anyone shows up to check on what's left of the facility."

Xavier nodded, "Yes indeed. Give Logan three more pills and give me the remaining two."

Once again Martinez handed Xavier two pills, gave Logan the rest and waited.

After a few minutes, Logan stirred, "Son of a bitch, my head is killing me, where the hell are we?"

Martinez looked on in surprise as Xavier put his sword back in the scabbard, locked it, and slowly rose to his feet. "What the hell are in those pills?" she asked.

"Never mind that," replied Xavier as they hoisted Logan to his feet, "We need to get to the car and get the hell out of here."

CHAPTER THIRTY-SIX

Drive to the Middle of Nowhere

The sky had turned shades of purple and blue that mixed with the orange haze of a setting sun, as the car continued it's trek through the desolate landscape. Martinez stared at the mesas and bluffs that littered the horizon, occasionally glancing at the screen of the GPS that had been hidden beneath a panel of the dash. Her hands ached as she held the wheel. Her adrenaline had started to fade, leaving her to feel the results of the ordeal they had just been through. She had never felt so totally wiped out in her entire life. The steady ache in her head told her she was probably concussed but, as she glanced at her two passengers, it was obvious she was the only one in any shape to drive.

Logan laid in the backseat and hadn't moved in the last forty five minutes, his occasional snoring the only sign of life. Whatever boost he had gotten from the mysterious pills had faded by the time they got to the car and he had passed out almost immediately. Xavier had flipped open the panel in the dash, punched in some coordinates, and spent the rest of the time just staring out his open window. He still looked like death itself, caked in blood, bruised and paler than any living person should be. Martinez was feeling worse by the minute, her stamina reaching its limits. It had almost become a robotic task at this point, sheer willpower forcing her to look at the road, glance at the screen, glance in the rearview at Logan. Over and over she repeated this routine, focusing all her energy on staying awake. It was at the end of one of these repetitions that she felt an odd feeling and glanced over to notice Xavier's steely eyes staring at her from the passenger's seat. The lights of the dash caused his already pale skin to glow, and it may have just been a trick of light, but his eyes appeared to have sunken deeper into the shadows of his face. She quickly glanced back to the road.

"Are you okay to continue driving?" Xavier asked in a low voice, his gaze locked onto her.

"Yeah, I'm okay," she replied, "besides, who else is going to drive if I don't? We don't have many options."

Xavier nodded and consulted the screen. "It's much appreciated, we shouldn't have much further to go."

"So what's our destination? When we got in the car we were in such a hurry that I didn't have time to ask," said Martinez as she too glanced at the GPS.

"We have safe points where there are secure lines that we can call to request backup, supplies, report in, things of that nature," replied Xavier, as he returned his gaze to the horizon.

They drove on a little longer and the silence grew, Martinez kept thinking over and over about what had happened during the standoff and the strange text message they had received. She didn't know why, but she was nervous to tell Xavier about it. The silence continued on and she couldn't think of a way to broach the subject. Finally, she cleared her throat and the words came tumbling out.

"So, during the gunfight we had while you were downstairs, the fighting was interrupted and a cell phone was slid to us. Whoever was on the other end claimed to be from the Citadel, whatever that is, and they offered myself and Logan five million dollars each if we would help them obtain the virus." She glanced over and saw Xavier had tensed up ever so slightly, his grip on the door seeming to tighten as he did.

"Do you have any idea who the Citadel is? Have you ever heard of them?" asked Martinez.

Xavier nodded almost imperceptibly, "Indeed," he said as he let out a slow sigh. "They are my employer."

Martinez felt her stomach drop and she glanced at Xavier with a look of disbelief on her face, "What the actual fuck? Are you serious? Then why are we going to a 'safe location' to check in? Isn't that the very definition of a bad idea?"

For a few seconds the silence grew again, and Martinez felt her impatience grow along with it. Xavier seemed to wrestle with a decision before finally tapping his hand on the vinyl panel of the door, "Okay fine, you might as well hear the whole thing while I'm still alive to tell it."

"The Citadel is made up of a large number of 'stations' scattered all over the world, they are interwoven into every nation on Earth and together they form a vast network. They have enormous resources and have influenced major world events for decades. My original orders were to obtain the virus, take it to a lab and destroy it. However, once I obtained the virus, I received a different set of orders, from a different 'station', instructing me to deliver the virus to a safe house. This struck me as odd, so I took it upon myself to defy the orders and have the virus destroyed anyway."

"And again, why do you think it's a good idea to go report in?" said Martinez, her knuckles starting to turn white as she gripped the wheel.

"It is my strong belief that the station that gave me the new orders were attempting some type of power play, that is, they were going to use the virus to gain more control over the entire organization. With the virus gone, I'm hoping that everything will return to the status quo." Xavier glanced over as he finished, noticing the tension that was building in Martinez.

After a few moments she shrugged her shoulders, "Okay, so what is the plan at this point, since your employer just tried to have us killed and all you have to go on is a hunch?"

Xavier rubbed his forehead, trying to will away a dull ache that was slowly growing into a roar inside his head. "Well, I honestly think it's going to go one of two ways, if my theory is correct then the power play will have now been crushed. They have no virus, they have no leverage. Once that happens we should be able to get a med team sent to us and in the long run, you and Logan should have your job situation straightened out."

Martinez glanced over at the pale figure next to her, "And what if you're wrong?"

"If I'm wrong, you'll get the keys to this car, several safety deposit box keys and locations, a bank account number to use, and you'll be the only one to leave the desert on this night."

They sat in silence as the night grew darker, like fate's shadow looming over them, "No. No fucking way. No I won't leave Logan, he's my partner and after everything we've been through I'm sure as hell not leaving you either."

Xavier reached over and quieted Martinez by resting his hand on her shoulder. "Agent Martinez, your loyalty is touching, but if things go south that is the only way it can go down. It's better that at least one of us makes it out of here and gets to go on living."

She turned and caught his eye staring into hers, "Let's face it," he said, with eyes that seemed to glow eerily in the dashboard lights, "If no help is coming, if there's no medical team, then Logan and I are already dead."

With that Xavier released her shoulder and went back to staring out the window. Martinez shuddered as a shiver went down her spine. She stared at the horizon and glanced at the GPS as the night grew quiet. After a few minutes she glanced back over at Xavier and was surprised to see he had apparently drifted off to sleep. She turned back to the road and eventually shifted back into her rhythm.

Look at the road, glance at the screen, glance in the rearview at Logan...

CHAPTER THIRTY-SEVEN

Cold Hand on My Back

She was so into her rhythm that she almost missed their destination. The GPS pinged and she slowed the car, wondering what she was supposed to see. Then off to the right on a barely noticeable road, covered by years of desert sand, sat what was left of an old service station. The main building looked to be barely standing and the gas pumps had succumbed to the harsh elements. Several picnic tables and a pay phone sat off to the side of the parking lot, which was rutted and cracked with a scattering of weeds. As Martinez eased the car into the deserted parking lot, trying her best to slowly go over the ruts, as to not shake her passengers, Xavier stirred from his slumber. As soon as the car stopped, Xavier opened his door and swung his legs out to the side gingerly.

"Stay with Logan, I'm going to go put a call in to my handler, I shouldn't be long."

Martinez nodded, put the car in park and sat staring at the rundown lot, feeling like a fool for having not driven back toward town instead. Why weren't they at a hospital? Why had they driven to the middle of nowhere? Her partner was dying in the back seat and they were off in some godforsaken place instead of getting medical care. She rubbed her forehead and let those thoughts dissipate   like she wished her headache would, but it stayed stubbornly in the forefront, not allowing her to rest for an instant. Her hearing was still half shot from the explosion and the never ending gunshots from earlier, her body battered and bruised and, more than anything else, she just wanted to stop. If this didn't work, she wasn't even sure if she had the endurance to get in the car and just drive. All she wanted was for it to end. She slumped her head on the steering wheel and closed her eyes.

With some effort, Xavier sat down onto the dusty picnic table, a shooting pain flaring up in protest from his side. The pain swelled to a crescendo and Xavier spent several minutes controlling his breathing to get the pain back under control. Once it had dulled back down to the ever present dull pulsing ache, he pulled a TracFone out of his jacket pocket, flipped it open, and dialed the number. Once he heard the familiar tone on the other end, he entered a three digit code and hung up. Several seconds went by, then a minute, then two. This was longer than he had ever had to wait on a response and Xavier started to get a sinking feeling of dread that his instinct had failed him as well as the two agents who had risked everything to help him. Just as he had started to give up hope, the pay phone beside the picnic table rang. After two rings, Xavier answered the phone. David's voice chimed in on the other end.

"Xavier? It's good to hear from you. I thought we might have lost you."

"You still may, my friend. I'm calling in to report that the mission is complete, Tears of the Dragon has been destroyed,"he waited as David seemed to pause.

"Very good," replied David, " Just for the record, and this is being recorded, as is normal protocol, are you confirming that your mission parameters, as originally laid out to you are complete and the target virus, Tears of the Dragon, has been completely eradicated?"

Xavier nodded to himself, "Yes, this is Xavier Greene and I am confirming that mission parameters have been completed, including the elimination of the virus known as Tears of the Dragon."

After he was finished, Xavier added, "David, are we good?"

Another uncharacteristic pause followed, Xavier could hear keys clacking on a keyboard. "That remains to be seen. But I will report to the original station from which this assignment came, and will call you back when I have a reply."

"Please hurry. We're in urgent need of a medical evacuation. Myself, as well as one other, are approaching critical condition and I'm not sure how much longer we can last."

There was no pause this time. "Understood Xavier. As I'm sure you are aware, I can't approve a medical evacuation until I get confirmation from above. But I'll hurry and will let you know as soon as I can." The phone clicked dead and Xavier sat pressing it's cool back against his forehead before finally hanging it up. He could feel his fever growing and the chill that came with it. He looked out across the night and felt the coolness of the dry desert air as a slight breeze blew across the plain. His adrenaline was gone, his reserves spent and at last, even he was out of tricks to prolong their lives. He knew the cold he felt wasn't just the night air or his fever, the cold he felt was the coming of death itself and even if the mission results were accepted, it might all be too late. He felt a shiver run through his body, the cold taking it's hold over him, the last of his warmth starting to drain out, like the blood he had already left on the floor of the lab. He glanced back at the car. Martinez had gotten out and was stretching her back, leaning up against the car. From the movement he could make out, it appeared Logan was awake again and they were talking quietly about something. He truly appreciated their help, but at the same time hated that they had to be involved. Two lives that, if not ruined or lost as the case may be, were at least irrevocably changed, not to mention they both had now gotten a glimpse of a far larger, and scarier world than they ever knew existed. In particular, he had told Martinez more than he had ever told anyone outside of the organization. He would have to keep this to himself, because the kind of knowledge she was carrying would be seen as problematic by people above him.

Suddenly he was jolted out of his thoughts, as the phone beside him rang.

CHAPTER THIRTY-EIGHT

Under the Milky Way

Martinez leaned against the car, staring off into the vast starry sky, breathing in the cool night air in hopes that her nerves would finally calm. Three days ago she was sitting in Starbucks enjoying a latte. Now she wasn't sure whether or not she was going to be a fugitive for the rest of her life. She couldn't wrap her head around the entire thing and the aching welled up inside her to the point she thought she would burst. She fought back tears, knowing that she needed to stay strong. She had already decided that even if Xavier's plan fell through, she had to figure out a way to save her partner, there was no way she could leave him here, no matter what.

"Uh yes, I'd like a double cheeseburger, fries and a chocolate shake please."

A grin crept cautiously across Martinez's face as she turned to see Logan leaning slightly out the window, his arm draped across the door, a slight, cocky grin on his face.

"How long have you been awake?" asked Martinez.

"Hell, I'm not sure I'm awake now. I can't feel half my body and the half I can feel, I would rather not. Given the shape I'm in, I have no idea how I'm even conscious," replied Logan before briefly falling into a coughing fit. He covered his face with the crook of his elbow and when he pulled his shirt back there were flecks of blood on it. "Well shit..." he muttered.

"You can thank our mysterious friend for that," Martinez replied. "He gave you something and took some himself, but judging from the looks of things, his tricks may have reached their limits."

Logan glanced at Xavier, who was sitting on a picnic table across the lot from them. "Yeah I was going to ask, where the hell are we? I hadn't put much thought into it, but I had kind of expected to wake up in an emergency room or something. What's he doing sitting over there by himself?"

Martinez shrugged, "Apparently he is negotiating for our lives, quite literally. The group that offered us all that money were apparently a faction of the same group he works for. He seems to think it may work out, but I've got my doubts."

Logan scratched his chin, "His own people huh? The same ones that offered us the money?"

"Yeah, why? Are you having second thoughts about not taking the money when we had the chance?" replied Martinez as she cautiously tried to stretch her tender back.

Logan continued to rub his chin for a minute and replied, "Nah. Like I said, five million is a lot of dough, but I wouldn't be able to sleep at night knowing that somewhere out there someone had that virus."

Martinez smirked at her partner, "Yeah I get that, besides, given the circumstances, who's to say they ever intended on giving it to us anyway? They could've just shot us in the back once they got what they wanted."

Martinez scuffed the dirt with her shoe, staring at the barely visible ground for a few moments before building up the nerve to broach a topic she hated to even bring up.

"So… if Xavier can't work things out with his people," she started, her voice faltering slightly under the weight of what she was about to say, "He wants me to take the car, with some money and supplies that he will tell me how to access, and leave you both out here to die."

Logan fought back another short cough and chewed on his lip for a few moments. "I actually agree with him. If it's a lost cause, then you should leave. I'm on borrowed time as it is and I'm sure he is just as bad off as me, if not worse. If he wants to give you a fighting chance, I'm all for it. Promise me you'll do it, if it comes to that."

Martinez shook her head, her brow furrowed into a knot as she fought back her emotions, " No way. I'm not going to agree to, or promise you anything. We'll do what we always do and figure it out. The only thing I will promise you is that you owe me a ton of drinks for getting us into this mess." She looked down to find Logan fighting back a chuckle.

"Okay fine. I'll pay up, provided we make it out of this mess alive, and with a job, so I can afford that legendary bar tab you're going to run up." At this they both broke into a laugh, sitting and having a drink at some bar seemed like such an unimaginable scenario, so far away and unattainable. But their mirth was cut short by a coughing fit that doubled Logan over, spitting blood on the back of the seat as he coughed. Martinez grabbed his shoulder to help steady him and when he finally settled he slumped back in the seat, his face a pale white.

"I may have to take a rain check on those drinks..." he mumbled as he seemed to slip from consciousness. Martinez stood, still holding his shoulder, and instinctively reached up to feel his pulse. It was still there, although she had to admit it was a lot weaker than she would like. Why couldn't they have driven into town? Her partner was lying here dying, and the helplessness she felt was about to rip her in two. Just then she glanced up and saw Xavier waving at her from the table. She glanced at Logan once more and walked over. As she approached, she noticed that Xavier seemed even more ghostly than on the ride over. Maybe it was a trick of light, but his pale skin seemed to sag with the effort of being upright.

"Good news," Xavier started in a raspy, wheezing voice that caught Martinez off guard. "The power struggle collapsed once the word got out that the virus was destroyed. I can't say much but the assassination of a major head of state will make the news in the next day or so and you can connect the dots yourself. Also a story is in the process of being circulated in regards to yourself and Agent Logan, with the approval of your bosses. You were both working under cover trying to infiltrate a bio terrorist cell. Reporters eager for a story published it before receiving the whole truth and unfairly accused the two of you of being terrorist yourselves." Xavier paused to catch his breath, which rattled emptily in his lungs, "Subsequently, you will hear about a prominent reporter being fired in the next few days."

"That's great!" Martinez exclaimed with relief, "But what about you two?"

Xavier breathed for a moment, seemingly marshaling his strength to reply, "A medical evacuation unit has been dispatched," Xavier wheezed, "it should arrive in about forty five minutes."

"Forty five minutes? No disrespect, but I'm not sure either of you are going to last that long."

Xavier nodded his head. "Regardless, that is what we have to deal with. Go back to the car and do what you can to keep Logan alive. There are blankets in the back of the car." Xavier replied.

"What about you?" asked Martinez.

"I'm going to stay right here, I don't think I have the strength to stand." With that Xavier sighed deeply and coughed for a few moments before slowly reclining onto the table. Martinez walked back to the car to tell Logan the good news but found he was still unconscious. Checking the back hatch of the car, she found the blankets and, after spreading one over Logan, she took another blanket back out to the table on which Xavier still laid prone. He didn't acknowledge her presence and if it hadn't been for the slight rhythm of his chest, she might have thought it was too late. Quietly she spread the blanket out and laid it over him. As she walked away she looked back over her shoulder and felt a shiver travel down her spine. With the blanket laying over him on the table, it now resembled some type of death shroud. Shaking her head, she walked back to the car to check on Logan.

A few moments later, Xavier's eyes opened once again, focusing on nothing but the moonless sky. The remoteness of their location offered a spectacular view, that were it not for the dire circumstances that they found themselves in, would be an absolutely breathtaking spectacle. Above them the stars shined bright with the Milky Way itself spreading from horizon to horizon. Xavier found himself marveling at the immense number of stars and the vastness of it all. He thought of all the people going about their normal lives the last few days, not knowing how close they came to losing it all. In the grand scheme of things his life is but one in a sea of many. What is it to lose his life in comparison to the genocide they had prevented? After a few moments Xavier felt a calm come over him and he felt at ease. With the success of this mission he, in all likelihood, saved the life of most of the population of this planet. If his life was the price paid to accomplish that, then it was worth it. He relaxed and felt the calm spread throughout his body. The dragon was dead, the world was safe, and he was at peace. For a few more moments Xavier laid watching the stars above him, then he closed his eyes and slipped into unconsciousness.

CHAPTER THIRTY-NINE

Phillip Dubois to the Rescue

Martinez checked her watch, it had been nearly forty minutes since she returned to the car. She had tried laying on the hood for a while, absorbing what little heat it had left, but she found her nerves wouldn't let her. Eventually, after checking on Logan and finding him still breathing, she had resorted to just pacing back and forth beside his window. She stopped again to check his pulse and it was then she noticed the rumble. It was low at first, barely noticeable, but it steadily grew as she listened. She glanced around, scanning the horizon and finally spotted a set of headlights approaching from afar. She watched as the mammoth lights approached their position, turning at the unmarked road with no hesitation and pulling into the small parking lot. As it pulled in she could now see that it was an absolutely gigantic eighteen wheeler, with an oversized trailer. Despite the small size of the parking lot, it easily swept around and stopped less than ten feet from the car. It's huge engine, as well as the sound of the air brakes being applied, shattered the still night air. Once the dust had settled an array of lights came on, temporarily blinding Martinez and illuminating the entire parking lot like it was midday. As her eyes slowly adjusted and she saw a door open on the side of the trailer just as a set of stairs automatically unfolded to the ground. The door swung open and out stepped the tallest man Martinez had ever seen. He was of Jamaican descent with close cropped hair, a white lab coat and shiny black shoes that reflected the glow of the lights. He adjusted his glasses, consulted his clipboard, and surveyed the scene before striding down the steps and approaching Martinez, his open hand outstretched.

"Agent Martinez?" he asked in a booming voice that carried even over the roar of the diesel engine, "Phillip Dubois at your service!"

His massive hand engulfed hers as he shook it. "I'm so glad to see you guys, I was starting to think you were going to be too late," said Martinez.

"Oh, no ma'am, there is no reason to worry, now that we're here everything is going to be just fine." He beamed a positively brilliant smile as he put a hand on her shoulder. "You have all been through a lot, now just relax and leave it all to us."

Almost as if on cue, the back of the trailer opened and a ramp extended down. Two teams of men with gurneys filed down the ramp, dressed in white scrubs and carrying bags of equipment.

"Team one, over there!" exclaimed Phillip, pointing toward the picnic table. "Team two, " at this he glanced around momentarily before spotting Logan, "over here. He is in the car."

Martinez marveled at the efficiency of the two groups. The first team immediately approached Xavier and pulled back the blanket. After checking his vitals and glancing under his jacket, they immediately placed an oxygen mask over his face, lifted him gently, slid him onto a gurney, covered him with a cloth, and quickly wheeled him away into the back of the trailer.

The second team opened the back door of the car and as one of the men examined Logan's leg, the other two opened the door he was laying against, while gently supporting him, so he didn't fall. Once the door was open they began checking his vitals, and assessing the situation. Finally, they slid him out of the car and onto a gurney, where he was also fitted with an oxygen mask and wheeled into the truck. The entire operation had taken less than four minutes. Martinez stood next to Phillip, who was supervising the entire thing, amazed at the coordination   displayed by the teams. Once the two gurneys were loaded back on the truck, another couple of men emerged and approached Phillip and Martinez. The men reached for Martinez, but she pulled back her arm.

"No thanks, I'm fine, you guys worry about the other two, they need it far worse than I do." The men paused, glancing up at Phillip. Martinez looked back and forth between the men and Phillip, who continued to look at her with a comforting smile.

Once again he placed a massive hand on her shoulder, "Come, come my friend. You have all suffered, but it is okay now. Your friends will be taken care of, but we mustn't neglect you either. Please go with these men and let them help you. Once your check up is complete, you can meet me in the main room and I will answer any questions you may have."

Martinez looked up at the gentle giant of a man and then over at the two men, who waited patiently. Finally she nodded her head and walked away with the men.

"Excellent," Phillip beamed, "they will take exceptional care of you! I will see you in a few minutes, we just have to take care of a few last details."

As Martinez walked to the ramp they were passed by several of the crew as they carried some equipment and approached Phillip. At his instruction they removed all of the valuables from the car, working meticulously and even checking all the secret compartments that were installed in it. Afterwards they looked over the picnic table, removing the blanket and finding the sword that Xavier had left laying beside it.

"Save that," said Phillip, pointing at the sword, "Our patient would be plenty angry if he lost it."

One of the techs took the sword and put it with the rest of the valuables in a large crate and carried it into the trailer. The remaining group carried the blanket and picnic table and piled it on top of the car. At Phillip's signal one of the techs took a sprayer wand and began covering the car with liquid accelerant. When he had completely soaked it, he stepped back, while another tech stepped up with a small flamethrower. After a nod from Phillip, the tech torched the car and table, which were instantly engulfed in flames. The techs returned to the truck and the ramp retracted. Phillip Dubois stood watching the fire for a few moments before checking his watch and smiling a brilliant smile. He consulted his clipboard, "Excellent! Less than nine minutes onsite. Excellent indeed." He turned and walked back up the steps and, ducking his head, stepped through the doorway. As he closed the door, the steps retracted, and the spot lights went out. Thanks to the accelerant, the fire had already mostly burned through the car and table, leaving only a burned out husk, the fire dying quickly. The truck's air brakes released and with a smooth, large turn, the truck slipped back out onto the road and into the night, like it was never there.

CHAPTER FORTY

In Good Hands

After her check up, Martinez sat on the table in the small examination room and rubbed her temples. The techs had given her the once over, patched up a few minor nicks and cuts, as well as given her some meds to help with her head and nerves. She had refused an x-ray so they wrapped her ribs as a precaution and warned her that in all likelihood she had suffered a concussion, but that otherwise she was fine. They had also left her a fresh pair of scrubs to change into if she wanted.

Eventually she got to her feet and walked over to a small sink, where a bar of soap and washcloth were laid out. Stacy Martinez stood and surveyed herself in the mirror.

"God you look like shit," she thought, as she looked at the myriad of bruises on her arms, neck, and face. She had been through some tough missions before, but this was beyond anything she had ever faced. She was sore, hadn't slept, and had been pushed totally beyond anything she had ever experienced. She stood there in front of the mirror, hands on the sink to brace herself for what felt like an eternity. Slowly she felt the throbbing in her head subsiding and the knots in her gut untying, no doubt both were due to the meds she had been given. She turned on the water, picked up the soap and washcloth, and started slowly scrubbing away at the road dirt on her face and arms.

A short while later she emerged from the door into the main room dressed in her scrubs and wearing some padded sandals. The main room was about twice the size of the examination room and featured a row of cabinets with various microscopes, centrifuges and computers on it. At one end of the room was a station where Phillip Dubois sat hunched over a computer, studying a report. He saw Martinez and immediately rose to meet her.

"Agent Martinez, how are you feeling?" he asked as he led her to an alcove at the back of the room. It contained a white circular table and several chairs. Phillip pulled out a chair and offered it to her. Martinez sat down as Phillip rounded the table and sat down across from her in a chair that looked comically too small for his large frame.

"I'm feeling better, thank you. I think at some point I may even feel human again," she replied.

Phillip smiled one of his gigantic smiles, "That is wonderful, I saw from your medical report that you had minor injuries, with the exception that you may have broken ribs, but you refused x-rays," with that he frowned slightly, "Are you sure? We have state of the art equipment here and give only the best care."

She shook her head, "I appreciate it, but I'm fine. It's not a big deal and even if they are broken, it's not my first rodeo."

With that Phillip nodded his head as he pondered a thought before replying, "Very well. Such a strange phrase that is, 'Not my first rodeo...'" He chuckled, "I may have to borrow that one."

Martinez interrupted his musing, "I hate to be pushy, but what about the others, how is Logan? How is Xavier?"

Phillip spread his large hands on the table, "Of course, of course. Your friends are getting treatment currently. Mr. Greene is in our surgery suite, currently undergoing multiple operations. His injuries are severe, but I have faith in our doctors, they will do their absolute best to ensure he pulls through." His brow furrowed, "However, I am puzzled by one thing. As I have stated both Mr. Greene and Agent Logan's injuries were severe and after looking at the reports, if I'm being honest, they should both be dead. I am at a lost to explain how they are here at all."

Martinez leaned forward in her chair, "You'll have to ask Xavier about that, if he pulls through. He had a pouch with some pills that he administered to himself and Logan. Every time either one of them took one it appeared to miraculously revive them. He also had some sort of salve that he applied to the wounds. I've never seen anything like it."

Phillip's eyes widen as he listened to Martinez's explanation. "Fascinating. Absolutely fascinating. I will have to question Mr. Greene, once he recovers. This could be a great advance for the medical world. He is always full of such surprises."

"So you've known him for a while?" asked Martinez, her curiosity getting the better of her.

Phillip rubbed his chin for a moment before replying, "Let's just say this is not our first rodeo..." before bursting into a large grin, proud of his use of the phrase.

Martinez smiled in spite of herself at his amusement, "Fair enough, that's what I get for asking," then with a more serious expression she followed up, "What about Logan?"

Phillip nodded, "Agent Logan did excellent. We cleaned his wound and packed it temporarily. He was given a transfusion, but he is still a little low, so we have stabilized him and are preparing to transfer him to a local medical facility. We are on route there now."

"Transferring to a local facility? I thought you guys were state of the art?" asked Martinez, her concern for her partner growing.

Phillip nodded his head, "Indeed we are. Mobile Medical One is the state of the art mobile medical unit, however we only have one surgery bay, which is occupied by Mr. Greene, so we cannot operate on Agent Logan. Besides, we were under strict orders to only stabilize him and drop him off at a medical facility, which I am sure is completely capable of completing the work that we have started."

"Ordered to stabilize him only? Who ordered that?" asked Martinez, her annoyance growing by the second.

Phillip shook his head, "I'm sorry my friend, I am not at liberty to say. All I can tell you is that your friend is in stable condition and he will be well taken care of. Anything more than that is off limits." Martinez started to protest but he raised his large hands, quieting her. "Trust me when I tell you, that is not a rabbit hole you want to go down Agent Martinez. The less you know the better, the more you forget about everything you have seen, the better your life will be."

With that Phillip rose from the table and walked to a nearby fridge, "Where are my manners? Here, I am sure you could use some water, after all your time in the desert." He retrieved a bottle of water from the fridge and offered it to Martinez, who took it and drank down half the bottle in one gulp. She hadn't realized it but she was starting to feel seriously dehydrated and the cool water felt wonderful.

"Can I get you anything else?" asked Phillip as he stood gazing down at Martinez.

She sat for a few moments, taking another sip of water and debated pressing him for more information, but decided she wouldn't get the answers she was looking for so she shook her head.

"No, I'm fine, thanks."

Phillip smiled, "Very well then, you rest, I will go check on the status of our main patient." With that he bowed slightly and left the room.

As the sun rose over another hot Arizona day, Mobile Medical One pulled up in front of St Joseph's Hospital. The back of the trailer opened and a ramp extended, as it had before. Phillip Dubois and a team of technicians came down the ramp, pushing Agent Logan on a gurney with IV attached, followed by Agent Martinez. They were met in the parking lot by a team of medics and after speaking briefly with Phillip, the medics took the chart that he offered them and wheeled Logan into the ER. As his own team of techs returned to the trailer, Phillip turned to Martinez.

"This is the end of the line Stacy Martinez, I wish you and your partner a speedy recovery and a safe life."

Martinez shook his massive hand, "Thank you for everything, please tell Xavier thank you for everything, if he wakes up."

Phillip nodded, "I will, my friend and have faith, Mr Greene is in our capable hands." Then placing a hand on her shoulder he leaned in slightly, "But remember what I said, Ms. Martinez, the more you forget about the things you saw, the better your life will be. I say this with all sincerity and good intentions." He paused slightly, before releasing both her shoulder and hand, his smile returning, "Farewell Ms. Martinez, it has been a pleasure." With that he returned up the ramp and into the trailer. The minute he entered, the ramp withdrew, the doors closed and Mobile Medical One rolled off out of the parking lot and headed for the highway.

Martinez stood watching the truck disappear into the traffic, like a veil falling back over a secret world. The early morning breeze blew through her hair and with the sunrise's pink and purple hues it was like waking up from a bad dream. She stood watching the sunrise for a few fleeting moments thinking about Phillip's last bit of advice to her. She reached in her pocket and pulled out a crumpled certificate of title that she had grabbed from the dash of the car while they waited for medical help back in the desert.

"Here's to rabbit holes..." she said, as she returned the paper to her pocket and turned to go check on her partner.

Read on for the first chapter of 'The Osiris Initiative',
the second novel in the Xavier Greene Thriller series.

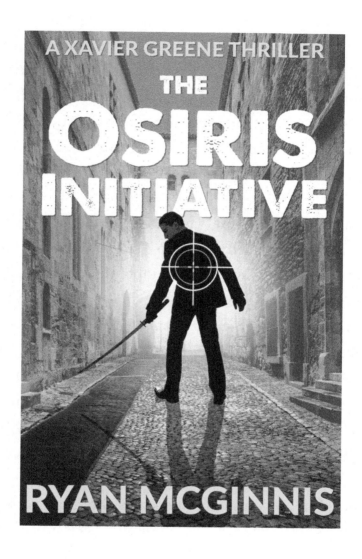

A XAVIER GREENE THRILLER

THE

OSIRIS
INITIATIVE

RYAN MCGINNIS

Citadel Safe House - Atlanta, Georgia

It was five-thirty when the alarm went off. Amy Kincaid rose and went through her routine of stretches and yoga, before taking a luxuriously warm shower. Afterwards she got dressed in her normal, white blouse, dark skirt and matching blazer. After appraising her appearance in her mirror, she pulled her blonde hair up in a bun and started downstairs. By six-thirty she was on the elevator on the way down from her top floor apartment. As the elevator glided down to the ground floor she made a cursory glance of the news headlines on her tablet before checking her schedule for the day. A new asset was due to arrive that afternoon but otherwise it looked like a quiet day. The asset they were currently hosting would be leaving by noon and not a moment too soon. They were under strict instructions to cater to the assets that were sent their way, but occasionally her limits were pushed too far. While she understood that these assets didn't live normal lives, some were impossible to deal with. She knew that they were mostly specialists, and occasionally assassins, that were paid big money to handle rather unique problems. Due to that type of lifestyle you were bound to get some eccentric types. However, the asset currently sleeping off his hangover in room three sixteen was too much. At first he seemed okay, very quiet and reserved. But after dinner he proceeded to get drunk at the bar downstairs. This in and of itself was not unusual. The problem began when he started smashing glasses on the floor and hitting on the bartender. If there was anything Amy liked, it was to run a tight ship. Everything has a place and everything should be in its place. All that she asked of their usual guests were for them to treat the residence, and the staff with respect. Security had gotten involved, of course, but when your guest is a world class assassin who's had way too much to drink, you have to handle these matters delicately. It was Amy herself who intervened and kept the situation from escalating. She swept into the room and defused the situation, offering to replace the bartender for the rest of the night. The asset was disappointed to see his current bartender go. But when Amy brushed her hand down his neck and let it play down his arm, he forgot all about his previous bar keep. She made him promise not to break any more glasses and in return, she would spend the rest of the night talking. Over the years, Amy learned that a lot of these assets just needed someone to listen. Most of them lead very lonely lives. They may have girlfriends and lovers in far away spots, but they rarely had anyone at home. It was a hard life and she understood that. She also understood that after letting them talk for a drink or two, a third drink laced with sleeping powder would do the trick and bring the night to an end without any hassle. Amy grinned thinking about how he would be none the wiser. He would just figure he drank until he passed out. Nice and neat, just how she liked it.

Amy strolled out of the elevator into the nerve center of the residence. Hidden away from the rest of the house were rows of security monitors and computer terminals. Around it was a gourmet kitchen, studies and offices, as well as a living room with plush couches. It was designed to be superior to the most luxurious hotels, a haven to their assets when they needed it. As she entered, her assistant, Alex, handed her a cup of hazelnut coffee with just a touch of cream, just the way she liked it. Alex was her right hand and she considered her essential to keeping the residence running smoothly.

Alex looked on as Amy paused to take a sip of her steaming mug of coffee, "So any update on three sixteen?"

Amy smirked as she looked at Alex over the steaming mug, "No. Last anyone checked he was sleeping it off in his room. We set a wake up call for ten and he should be out of here before lunchtime."

"I thought for sure we were going to have a serious situation last night."

Amy grabbed her tablet and coffee, "Just goes to show you just need to know how to handle them."

Alex fell in beside her as they started their rounds, "That's why you're the boss."

They made a stop by the bar to survey the damage from the night before. The glass had been cleaned up, but there were several large gashes in the hardwood floor and a cracked tile in front of the fireplace. Amy groaned to herself. The floor would be easy enough to fix, but those tiles were ordered from France especially for this room. A replacement was not going to be cheap. Looking up, she noticed a spot on the wall. She leaned over to examine it and found a stray piece of glass must have hit the wall, cutting a small gash in the wallpaper. She sighed as she looked at the Scalamandre Zebra wallpaper. They had gotten it specifically for the bar area to give it a big game, safari type feel. At over four hundred dollars per roll, with a two roll minimum, that was going to sting. She shook her head, three sixteen couldn't leave soon enough.

Amy turned to Alex, "Looks like we've got hard wood repair, a cracked imported tile, and some very expensive ruined wallpaper."

Alex winced, "The accountants are going to hate that. We'll have to be sure to charge it to his Station."

Amy agreed. Assets of the higher levels were considered subcontractors, of sorts. They couldn't just quit if they liked, even though a few had managed it. For the most part, they were at the beck and call of the various Stations. The Stations were all completely separate entities that operated under the Citadel. The leaders of each one shared high level information and occasionally consulted with each other, but otherwise they operated independently. They worked in harmony, although there were occasionally some problems. Amy thought back to that debacle last year. She hadn't heard anything officially, but the rumor was that one Station went rogue and tried to intercept a package from another Station. The asset involved, she believed his name was Xavier Greene, even stayed with them for a night. She didn't know how it ended, except that everything calmed down after a few weeks. She heard that the head of a Station was terminated, in a most final sense, but that was idle gossip. The truth was that whatever happened, only the people at the top knew for sure.

She was about to check her tablet for the next thing on their agenda when she got a call in her earpiece.

"Amy, this is security, I hate to bother you so early

but we've got an issue."

She pressed the earpiece to respond, "What's the problem?"

"The outside cameras just went offline. There were some problems the other week due to utility work in the area, so it may be nothing. But we're flying blind until we get it straight."

Amy bit her lip, it was highly unusual for the entire outside array to go down. "Okay keep me posted-"

Suddenly a huge explosion rocked the building. Over her earpiece Amy heard security calling out,

"Back door is breached, I repeat backdoor is breached."

At once the entire residence was thrown into chaos. Amy grabbed Alex by the arm and raced down the hallway.

She pressed her earpiece again, "Initiative security protocols, all non security staff get to the panic rooms immediately!"

Amy and Alex could hear the sound of small arms fire as they arrived in front of a large bookcase in the library, along with some of the rest of the staff. Each safe house was equipped with a series of panic rooms, where the staff would gather in case of a breach. Although they ran drills once a month, she never thought they would actually be needed. She didn't have time to worry about that now though, she had people to protect. She reached out and pressed the copy of 'War and Peace' on the third shelf. The bookcase swung open and they all ran inside, pulling the foot thick steel door shut behind them. Once inside, she locked the door. The release built into the bookshelf wouldn't work now. Now there were only two ways the door would open, if she opened it from the inside, or if someone entered the numerical password into a keypad hidden out in the library.

She took a quick survey of the room. There were eight of them in here, which left about twelve more staff members, not including the security force. Alex was already bringing the computers online and soon the monitors came to life. She saw the other panic rooms, each filled with the rest of the staff. She scanned the hallways and saw the backdoor gaping open from the explosion. She could see a bloody body laying in the rubble. She quickly changed the view, there would be time to mourn the dead later. Now she had to hold it together. She briefly caught a glimpse of a team of men in military garb, wearing black face masks and carrying assault weapons. Then the camera for the hallway cut out. One by one each of the cameras blinked out to static till all that was left were the other panic rooms. She was about to use the comm to call the other rooms and check in when one of the feeds cut to static. Amy stared at the monitor, wondering what the hell was going on. She turned to the cabinet in the back of the room and took out a key from her jacket. She opened the cabinet to reveal a small cache of handguns. She began handing them out to the rest of the staff.

Alex protested, "Amy, we're not soldiers, I've never even fired a gun."

Amy pressed the steel into her assistant's hand, "Now isn't the time to worry about that. I'm sure everything is fine. We just need to make sure."

She went back to the monitor and saw the other remaining panic room. Suddenly its feed also cut to static.

"What the hell is going on?" muttered Amy as she stared at the static. She reached for the emergency phone to try to ring the Station in control of the safe house, but when she put it to her ear, the phone was dead. She turned to Alex and gave her head a slight shake. Alex pulled out her cellphone.

"Damnit, we don't have a cell signal in here either!" complained Alex as she stared at her phone.

Amy turned back to the monitors and turned on the camera in the library. The black and white security footage of the room looked eerie and silent. Amy stared at the monitor, her blood pressure and heart rate slowly rising. A group of men appeared in the doorway. The same men in black with the paramilitary gear that she had seen in the monitor earlier. The distorted look of the security feed made them look like ominous phantoms, moving through the stark white room. To Amy's horror one of the men reached over and flipped open the keypad. It was hidden, there was no way they could have known it was there. The man punched in the code for the keypad and the light on the inside of the door switched from red to green. She could hear the hiss of the releasing hydraulic locks. Several of the staff tried to grab at the handle, desperate to hold the door shut. Amy raised her gun and pointed it at the door as it swung open. She never got the chance to pull the trigger. She hesitated, as they all did. And in their hesitation, they were lost.

Your Free Ebook is Waiting!

All they wanted was the perfect family...

Kevin and his wife Sam had the perfect life, all that was missing was a child. That changed when they met Lily. But parenthood is more than they bargained for. Every night brings new terrors, each worse than the first. Are they falling into a nightmarish decent into madness, or is there something more sinister going on?

Get a free copy of "A Good Night's Sleep" here:

ryan-mcginnis.com/good-nights-sleep-free-ebook

About The Author

Ryan McGinnis grew up reading Science Fiction, Horror, and Suspense Novels at the local library. Ray Bradbury, Kurt Vonnegut, and Ian Fleming all loomed large over his childhood. He has previously written the short story "Sketch", which is available on Mandatory Midnight, and "A Good Night's Sleep", which is available at his website, ryan-mcginnis.com.

Learn more and find out what is coming next at ryan-mcginnis.com.
For behind the scenes, early sneak peeks and exclusive bonus material, check out patreon.com/ryanmcginnis.

Made in the USA
Coppell, TX
27 March 2022

75613321R00108